A Word in Season

a collection of short stories

CREST BOOKS

The Salvation Army National Publications
Alexandria, Virginia

Published by Crest Books, Salvation Army National Headquarters
615 Slaters Lane, Alexandria, Virginia 22314
(703) 299–5558 Fax: (703) 684–5539
http://www.salvationarmyusa.org

Printed in the United States of America

Cover photo by Diane Tolcher
Cover design by Laura Ezzell
Sectional design by Henry Cao and Jennifer Williams
Composition by Jennifer Williams

Library of Congress Catalog Card Number: 2002116200

ISBN: 0–9704870–8–8

Unless otherwise noted, Scripture taken from the *Holy Bible, New International
Version.* Copyright 1973, 1978, 1984 by International Bible Society.
Used by permission. All rights reserved.

Some stories in this book appeared in slightly different versions in selected
issues of *The War Cry.*

The Salvation Army National Publications wishes to acknowledge Ariose Music
and EMI Music Services for permission to use lyrics from the song
"Every Season" by Nichole Nordeman.

Contents

Contents

Introduction

Jesus was not a theologian. He was God who told stories. The world of the Bible, both Old and New Testaments, is the world of story. Whether telling about a woman who lost a valuable coin or of a man who lost his son, Jesus taught the rich truth of God's great love through tales spun with beauty, grace, and courage.

The story holds rich variety and sparkling urgency. It is a clarion call to listen to the hunger in our deepest selves, to allow the story written in our hearts to emerge. It can then be a light to illumine our pathway home.

Stories have power to change us because they reach the whole person, not just the cognitive faculty. We read and identify with characters who demonstrate courage and self-sacrifice as we vicariously make choices along with them. In the process, our own character is shaped. As C. S. Lewis writes, "I become a thousand men, yet remain myself."

For every season of our lives, the story helps define our experience and move us beyond ourselves. Crest Books is proud to present *A Word in Season*—a collection of short stories, all of which have appeared at one time in the Salvation Army's periodical *The War Cry*. Some are factual accounts of historical events, such as "A Swedish Saga" by Brita Wicklund, which chronicles the adventures of one of the first Swedish Salvation Army officers to take an appointment in America. Stories like Max Lucado's "Resurrection Morning" from *Tell Me the Story* have great power to ennoble, challenge, and inspire as they broaden our understanding by drawing on the classics, history, science, and art. Other contributions in the collection recount stories that could have happened, or will yet happen, in the ongoing drama of human existence within the panoply of salvation.

Fiction is the world of story, which far from implying a lack of truth, rightly executed, carries truth to our meaning–hungry minds. Authors who write good fiction enrich us by making their learned life part and parcel of our own, offering us the rich diversity they have experienced.

William Faulkner spoke of the old universal truths "lacking which any art is ephemeral and doomed—love and honor and pity and pride and compassion and sacrifice." *A Word in Season* employs these same universal truths which make for real art. These stories have never grown cold or ceased to bring the light and inspiration we need to live in this and any age.

In a deeply unsettled culture, artists provide models of how to say something about one's experiences of the sacred when rational discourse comes up short. May the stories contained in *A Word in Season* enrich and ennoble your life and the lives of those with whom you share them.

LT. COLONEL MARLENE CHASE
Editor in Chief and Literary Secretary
The Salvation Army

Every evening sky, an invitation

to trace the patterned stars;

Early in July, a celebration

for freedom that is ours;

And I notice You in children's games,

In those who watch them from the shade;

Every drop of sun is full of fun and wonder.

White Sidewall Shoes

The outburst was unnecessary, but the day had been building up to some kind of explosion, and I let it rip.

"You nitwits have lost my luggage? What kind of half–baked operation are you running?" I shouted. I was mad, and about three hundred people in the hot airport in Port–au–Prince, Haiti, now knew it.

Looking back on the situation, I know the Haitian people couldn't help it; the U.S. airline had been at fault. But I made a fool of myself anyhow and attracted the attention of an airport representative. The baggage handlers spoke only their native Creole, but this uniformed supervisor addressed me with a smile and perfect English, Caribbean style, with a British accent.

"May I assist you to my office?"

Once there, he assured me that my luggage would come through later that day. Until then, I would be the guest of the airline at a downtown hotel in Port–au–Prince. At their expense, I was to shop for a suitable outfit and eat at one of the American–style restaurants nearby. I couldn't ask for more. Feeling more composed, I left the office.

It was then, just outside, that I saw the white sidewall shoes for the first time.

Joe stood smiling at me, his feet encased in homemade shoes with rough canvas tops and rubber soles from tires that still bore traces of their white sidewalls.

"That was easy, wasn't it?" he said in fairly understandable English.

"I beg your pardon?"

He smiled again. "Your tour group told me to stay here and tell you that they are on a bus headed for this restaurant." He handed me a card that read *Choo–choo Restaurant.* "I'm to take you there."

He led me outside. I followed the white sidewall shoes as we made our way through a wall of smiling Haitians. At the curb was a *tap–tap,* a pickup truck outfitted in the back with two benches for seats. This one had a solid top for protection and was colorfully decorated in yellows and reds with the words "Queen of the Seas" painted in bold letters on the sides.

It was a rough ride until we were out into open country—weaving in and out of traffic with the roar of near misses and the honking of horns from each car that came our way.

The Choo–choo restaurant was indeed a replica of a train yard with model electric trains circling the huge tables where customers sat. A German railroad man ran the place. And there sat my two dozen friends laughing and enjoying the colorful scenery and the chugging of model trains as they "served" the table.

As we entered, I asked my guide, "Will you eat here, too?"

Something about his face, something about his mouth, something in the soul of him showed through. "No, my Marie will be waiting." Joe's eyes scanned the room. Somehow I knew he had never eaten in a restaurant.

I took his arm. "Tonight Marie dines alone." I pulled him to the table and announced, "This is my friend, Joe, and he's my guest for tonight." Joe protested but I insisted. He ate in silence. The American food served by the small chugging trains was strange to him.

After the meal, I was about to give him my farewell and join the tour group for an evening in Port–au–Prince's nightlife when I again saw something in his eyes.

He motioned me aside. "How will I tell Marie?"

I was stumped. Then he asked, "Would you come with me and tell her?" He assured me that he would pay for the *tap–tap* to take me back to the nightclub to rejoin my friends.

A strange feeling came over me. I told my friends that I'd join them later. Then we were off. As we rode through the crowded streets, once again in the big city, I watched the throngs of people. They were poor—incredibly poor—but they also seemed happy.

Winding our way north and out of the city, we came to a spot in the countryside. There, the *tap–tap* stopped. We got out and walked down a dark dirt road. Finally, a door, a room, and more smiling faces.

Joe explained the evening's events in Creole, as I nodded. When my eyes became accustomed to the weak kerosene lamp, I could see that Marie and the three children were about to eat.

Joe said, "She says you must have coffee." Something compelled me to accept. A few more minutes wouldn't hurt.

They bowed in prayer; Joe prayed in English, "Thank You for this kind American who is so rich. Bless his family while he is here." I heard little else as I remembered my wife in the rehabilitation center for alcohol abuse and my daughter now on parole after being sentenced for drug dealing. *Yes, God, if You are there, help them. Help me.*

They ate, and I drank my coffee. We laughed as the children asked dozens of questions about America. Tourists had always been too busy to talk to them. Even Joe and Marie knew little about the world outside their country.

Joe explained that the family moved three years ago from a tiny village to find work closer to the city. They had heard that the sugar cane industry was hiring. Marie now works in a sugar cane factory, and Joe is employed by the Haitian Sugar Company as a helper on the train that runs to the cane fields. They were lucky. Then I remembered the shoes. Lucky, but not enough to buy a pair of shoes.

"We miss the village," Joe explained. "But we have Jesus and we are happy."

Oh, if only I could have that simple assurance of joy, I thought.

"We will go to the church tonight. Will you go with us?"

I didn't know what to say. Church? How long had it been? And here in this poor land? Those eyes of Joe's again—they got to me. Suddenly I had a longing to have the peace and joy and love that I felt in this tiny shack on the outskirts of Port–au–Prince.

"Yes, I'd like to go." Joe promised that he would escort me to the big hotel that night so I could rejoin my friends. So, we went.

The church was also crowded—again, wall–to–wall people.

Children sat on the floor, while their mothers stood or sat nearby. Some of the men sat, but most were standing. Still others stood in the doorway looking in, and the joy and laughter echoed all around.

Guitars appeared; Creole and French voices blended. Nothing was in English. But the same presence was in that place that I had seen in Joe's face—a peacefulness, a serenity, a calm assurance that someone else was in charge, a feeling that no matter what might happen—a catastrophe, physical danger, political revolution—nothing could shake the faith of these people.

It was marvelous. It was refreshingly like what I remembered from my home long ago. Then they started singing in Creole some of the songs we'd sung when I was a kid. I picked out "Only Trust Him" and "When the Roll Is Called Up Yonder." Then they began singing "Just As I Am." My heart couldn't take any more, and I wept.

They sang in Creole and I sang in English. The words, the spirit, the total impact of that song flooded my mind with memories of my mother's prayers. I saw that old church house in the country. How long ago? Thirty years? Forty?

I felt a hand on my shoulder. It was Joe's. "Sir, do you want my Jesus?" That was all he said.

To this day the words are burned on my heart. I turned, I saw those eyes, I felt them reach out. In a flash I was kneeling with Joe at a rough altar rail. Splinters tore at my arms, but I felt nothing. We prayed. I surrendered my life. Now, as I look back, all I can do is weep in amazement at the path God led me down that night. If I hadn't lost my luggage . . . if I hadn't seen those shoes . . .

The whole church then began to celebrate, singing and jumping around after the service. Suddenly, sodas appeared for everyone—I learned later that Joe had paid for them with half his weekly salary. As we headed home late that night in Joe's old truck, Marie sang and the children slept.

Then Joe stopped the truck by the side of the road. "You must decide," he said.

"What?" I asked.

"Your plan was to rejoin your friends."

"Yes."

"And what will they do? It is ten at night."

I thought. Then I saw what he meant. They would be in some nightclub until three in the morning. Then days of drinking and sightseeing. I was suddenly a stranger to my own people and a brother to a poverty–stricken Haitian. What could I do?

"I can't go back."

Joe started the truck again, and we lumbered along in silence.

"Brothers are to help," was all he said as we parked by his shack. With no explanation, no excuses, Joe fixed a place in the corner of the crude house. I only had a mattress of cane fiber and a much–mended blanket, but I slept like a baby.

Early the next morning I awoke to busy feet all around me. Before daybreak Joe and Marie were hard at work. Joe took me with him to the steam engine shed, and I rode all day on the cane train. It was three glorious days of spiritual and mental freedom. I learned to know and love little Jean, Hector and Jacques. Marie was so kind, so gentle, so thoughtful.

And Joe—nearly illiterate, poor, younger than I—Joe became my spiritual big brother. In his halting English he taught me as we rode the narrow–gauge rails. While the field workers loaded the train, he read to me from Paul and the Gospels.

Soon I had to say, "Joe, today my plane leaves for the U.S. I don't know what my fun–loving tour friends think has happened to me, but I must go." I pressed some money in Marie's hands. She wept. I then embraced Joe and we both wept. It was a long truck ride to the airport.

My tour group was boarding the plane as I approached the gate. After one last hug of Christian love, I pulled myself from Joe. Suddenly he thrust a package into my hands and was gone, slipping through the crowd with ease. I stood and watched him.

I overheard the tourists curse the incompetence of the airport workers; I noticed the laughter in the crowd as a poor man walked by with a hole in the back of his pants; a dirty, naked boy brushed one tourist's leg and was cursed in lurid English. My heart was heavy for these people, but I also felt sorry for my rude, intolerant tour mates. I prayed for strength and the wisdom I would need on the flight home to witness for Jesus to these needy, needy people. Then I opened the brown bag Joe had given me.

I reached in and took out a worn pair of white sidewall shoes and clutched them to my heart.

Dan Harman

The Plum Tree

She had picked the fruit and had given bagfuls to the neighbors, but Ellen saw that a few plums still clung to the highest branches. In the morning light the mockingbirds and blue jays were making a noisy picnic over them. Gazing out the window, Ellen remembered how nearly every August since she and Tom had planted that tree twenty years ago, it had supplied the neighborhood with plums. One year the weight of the fruit had split the tree in half. Tom had trimmed the broken trunk and . . . "Mom?"

She hadn't heard Jenny come threading her way through the boxes stacked on the floor. Ellen put her arm around her daughter, and together they stood at the window watching the birds.

After a while, Jenny said, "There aren't any plum trees there."

"No."

"I won't know anyone. I won't have any friends."

"Of course you will."

"Mom," she whispered as if imparting a great secret, "I don't really want to go."

But they had gone over it and over it; they had memorized their lines.

"We held on as long as we could," Ellen said methodically. "There was too much yard work, too much to keep up with. And the payments were too high."

She broke off. The real reason, the only important reason, was the last. Once again she felt the sickening surge of regret.

"Come on," she told Jenny. "Let's go make toast. Johnny will be here in a minute with the trailer. We'll have to pack the dishes."

That's right, she told herself. *Seem confident. Keep busy.*

Ellen was getting good at appearing confident. But at thirty–eight, she was just as frightened of the future as her youngest child was at seven. As for keeping busy—setting a goal and working toward it— that's what had led inexorably to this day and the troubled look in her daughter's eyes.

She held Jenny tightly, then turned away so that the child wouldn't see her face. For the thousandth time she wondered if there had been something else she could have done. *Couldn't I somehow have saved the home Tom made for us—where our memories are, where we've been happy?*

Johnny bustled in, flushed with the eldest–son importance of bringing back the rented trailer. The twelve–year–old twins, Joe and Marie, were up by now, and after a quick breakfast everyone went to work moving bit by bit into the small apartment across town. It was going to be crowded, even with some of their things placed in storage.

Ellen's troubled spirit made her slow and tired. With the second load she sent the children off alone, saying she needed time to pack the bedding and books. She wandered around the half–empty house, then sat on the stripped bed and took up the Bible that always lay on the night table. For five years, since Tom had died, it had been her greatest consolation.

She held the Book unopened, thinking of her husband, who, even during his illness, hadn't wanted her to work. She hadn't wanted to, either. But there had been little money and no insurance, and Ellen would soon be alone with four children to support. She had no choice.

Rather, her choice had been to take an unskilled job or to return to school and prepare for a future without Tom. Ellen had taken a part–time job as a teacher's aide and discovered that she loved to teach and was good at it. She had borrowed money on the house, signed up for as many courses as she could handle at a time, and then studied desperately hard. She had earned her teaching credentials and had found a job she loved. But it had all been so expensive. It would be years before her teacher's salary would make up for what she had spent.

Ellen was forced to borrow money on the house a second time. But the larger payments were more than she could meet every month, and there would be college expenses for Johnny next year. She tried to struggle with the loan payments but, at last, had to admit she was beaten. So, Ellen sold the house.

She missed Tom so terribly, and now there was a second sweeping loss to her family. Ellen opened the Bible, and the Book fell open to the verses that had always sustained her in the darkest times. But it opened there not only because she read those pages so often. Tucked between them was a scrap of paper. She must have placed it there but couldn't remember when.

She smoothed out the coarse, lined paper. It was from one of her kindergarten students. She remembered the boy. His arms were thin as sticks, and he was always falling asleep in class. His family had drifted out of town before the year was over—but not before Ellen had awakened in him an eagerness to learn. He had written her a letter. It read *I love you.* Above the words he had drawn a brilliant green tree studded with scarlet fruit. Apples? Or were they plums?

Suddenly in Ellen's mind the child's tree blended into another tree, and at last she received the message that God must have been trying to send her all day, ever since that morning when she stood watching the birds. Again she saw Tom trimming away the broken branches of the plum tree as she stood by helplessly. This time she heard his words.

"Don't worry about what's lost," he had said. "The tree may be lopsided for a while, but new branches will spring up to fill the empty place. God sees to it that things balance out."

The children returned noisily, their chattering and clattering reverberating from the empty walls.

Jenny was saying, "And my bed looks good there, the bedspread is just the right color. And I saw a girl on the street who might go to my new school, and . . ."

Ellen closed the book over the paper and looked up with a genuine smile, not a forced one.

Later, when the trailer had left with Johnny, and the final few items were packed and waiting with the kids in the car, Ellen asked her children to wait for just one more moment. She walked into the backyard, setting off an explosion of complaining birds from the plum tree. She touched the trunk for the last time.

Yes, the scars were still there. They would always be there. But with God's help they had healed. Around them was a circle of new branches.

The tree hadn't taken the shape originally intended. After its loss, it had grown in new directions. But it was a sturdy tree, a productive tree.

Ellen sent a prayer of thanks up through the green branches, and hurried away.

Willie Rose

Too Grand

Sarah Findley lifted a weather–beaten hat from its peg and stepped out into her backyard. She let the screen door flap dully in its frame, breaking the silence, which was never so severe in her carefully tended yard as in the solitary house.

Gladiolas, fire–red and white, lined the fence, and irises of all shades mingled to the borders of the twin gates. Salvia, snapdragons and ruffled petunias nestled in graduated rows, perfect complements to her tender nurturing. Something close to a smile touched the thin lips in her wrinkled face. It was the rigid smile of one who had forgotten what it was like to experience the kindness and fellowship of kindred souls.

Tucking wisps of wiry hair under her straw hat, she studied one flaming gladiola on its bright green stalk and stood watching. John would be proud of the care she had taken with his roses. The smile faded, and a familiar hardness spread over the features that seemed incongruous to the sunny surroundings.

Suddenly there came a whooshing sound, then a dull thud. Her quick eye had seen the ball fly over her fence and flop into the cupped face of a purple iris. Mrs. Findley rushed toward it, exclaiming in words she could not later have recalled and picked up the thing that had left her flower crushed.

In the same moment two small heads peered over the gate, fear clouding their pale faces, eyes wide with dread.

"My poor iris!" Mrs. Findley cried, cradling it as though it were a rare thing rather than one of hundreds in her garden. She strode angrily to the children who stepped back and ran toward their porch. "How many times do I have to tell you to keep that ball out of my flowers!"

She gave the thing an angry toss. The children scooped it up and disappeared around the corner of the house.

Trembling, Mrs. Findley carefully braced the injured stalk, talking to it all the while as though apologizing to a friend . . . or perhaps to her departed husband. She found it difficult to bring his face into focus, a thing that fretted her worse than the incident with the neighbor children. She supposed she couldn't expect children to understand how important the garden was to her. After all, it was all she had left of him.

After a cup of tea she resumed her careful weeding until the sun was high in the sky and her knees hurt from the continual kneeling. Among her flowers her heart felt some ease from its desperate loneliness. If only she could keep the kids and the animals out.

As she turned around she saw it sitting there, watching her, its bronze fur bright in the sunlight and its tail switching back and forth over the beds of delicate pinks.

"You again!" The cat was new in the neighborhood and had not yet learned to respect her garden, even though she had chased it away several times in the past week.

For answer the huge cat tipped its head this way, then that, as though enjoying some sort of game. Mrs. Findley went for her garden hoe but stopped abruptly. She would march that feline menace right over to its owners and demand that they keep it restrained. She knew every animal on the block, so this one had to belong to the new people who had moved into the Jenners' old place.

She gathered the cat up in her thin arms where it nestled contentedly, mistaking her disgust for attentiveness. Mrs. Findley knocked loudly and rapidly, unable to stand still and infuriated by the cat's purring. The irresponsibility of some people to utterly ignore the simplest laws of—

The door opened to reveal a young girl sitting in a wheelchair. Her face, surrounded by light auburn hair, was pale but full of the most pleasing light and energy.

"Oh, Morris. There you are!" the girl said fondly, holding out her arms.

Mrs. Findley stared transfixed while Morris wriggled to be free. The girl spoke again. "How kind of you to return him to me. I'm afraid he's something of a vagabond."

"Well—your cat—was in my flowers again," Sarah began, "and I really must insist—" She stopped short, arrested by the soft beauty of the child who must have been about twelve, fragile but as beautiful as a snowy hybrid rose.

"You have a garden?" the girl asked, her eyes growing large and luminous. "I've always wanted to have one with all kinds of flowers of every color and shape! Oh, can I see your flowers, Mrs.—Mrs.—"

"Findley," she supplied with some annoyance. "But I'm afraid it's way at the end of the block," she added, frowning at the iron chair.

"Oh, I can get around great," the girl said. "See?" With that she was out of the house and down the ramp onto the road in seconds.

"My mother says people who grow flowers are generous people, and they always have something to give away."

Mrs. Findley did not respond but opened the twin gates to the yard.

"Oh, how beautiful!" the girl breathed, as though she were viewing the Queen's Royal Gardens. After several minutes of exclamation and moving from one end to the other of the garden, the girl's shining eyes held Mrs. Findley's. "What do you do with so many beautiful flowers?" she asked simply.

"I take care of them," she responded stiffly.

"I mean after that," the girl urged with excitement. "What fun it would be to pick armfuls of them and—"

"Oh, no, we mustn't pick them. They're—they're too grand for that," Sarah ended feebly.

For answer the girl only looked at her in great puzzlement. Shortly she wheeled around. "If they were mine I would gather them in great bouquets and take them wherever people were sad."

Soon the child went home to leave Sarah Findley strangely unnerved and depressed. She thought a long time about the girl, about her flowers and her own peculiar emptiness. Her mood varied from irritation to wondering to shame. She had determined to ignore the reproaches of a simple disabled girl, but the memory of her shining eyes and her noble spirit accompanied her through the warm days of summer—days when the young girl could frequently be found admiring the beautiful flowers at the end of the block.

That the child grew steadily more pale and more easily wearied Sarah did not notice, perhaps because she had been seldom in any but her own company and that of the flowers.

"Mrs. Findley, why do you think God made so many kinds of flowers?" she asked one day.

Mrs. Findley couldn't imagine, but the girl answered her own musing. "I think it's because He made so many different people. There's surely one flower to please everyone."

Two days passed and the girl did not come. Mrs. Findley reminded herself that she was favored to be rid of the annoyance. Still, she ended up returning to the old Jenner place. Morris had come without the girl—come to sit on her petunias, defying her warnings. Now she muttered to the cat as she waited at the door.

A tall woman looking much in the face like the girl only with soft touches of gray at her temples responded to her ring.

Mrs. Findley clicked her heels together. "Your daughter's cat, ma'am—I'd thank you to keep it away from my garden—" As she spoke, her eyes scanned the room and hallway beyond for some sign of the child and her chair, but there was a somber silence in the house.

"I see," the woman murmured. Then, as though interpreting Mrs. Findley's agitation, she said, "Carole won't be coming back this summer. She'll have to spend the next few months in the hospital again." Here the woman's voice caught and her eyes dropped momentarily. "In fact, I was just now on my way to the city to be with her."

Sarah could not have explained the sense of loss that washed over her. Something of greatness—of beauty had suddenly been drawn away. The words caught in her throat.

"Oh, I'm terribly sorry," she murmured, still foolishly hoping to see Carole's bright eyes. "I'm sorry—" She turned as if to leave, then paused briefly.

Mrs. Jenner spoke again. "I don't suppose you know someone who could look after Morris? I can't keep him in the city and if Carole should return—" She broke off perhaps in response to a stricken look she saw creep into Sarah Findley's eyes. "That is, when she—"

A quietness stretched between them. Then Sarah cleared her throat and held out one well-tanned arm. "Morris can stay with me temporarily, I'll take good care of him, and perhaps I can teach him not to sit in the petunias." With that she scooped up the furry bundle and left, walking very fast and very tall. That way a woman could outwit heartache, couldn't she?

Once back in her own yard she set Morris down and began gathering stalks of iris and gladiolus, sprays of roses and honeysuckle until an enormous bouquet filled her arms. If she hurried she could send them off with Carole's mother.

With a sense of gladness and life such as she had not known in years she latched the gate with a last reminder to her new companion, a reminder that sounded much less stern than she could have known. "Not in the flower beds, Morris, anywhere but the flower beds."

Wizened Sarah Findley dabbed at a stubborn trickle on her cheek. "My flowers," she continued, "are much too grand for that."

And in her heart she thought she could hear a soft whisper, whether of her own or another's she could not tell, "But they are not too grand to give away!"

Lt. Colonel Marlene Chase

The Captain Loved Jesus

Not a single pair of more forlorn–looking waifs than eight–year–old Anna Almeira and her younger sister Maria could have been found in all of Brazil. And this was not because their days were a never–ending treadmill of work. They were used to work. They had toiled, sunrise to sunset, in the fields with their parents and five brothers since they were babies. But after the new baby died, their mother never went to the fields again. She lay on her bed with scarcely enough strength to drink the cup of weak coffee, which Anna would hold to her mother's lips. For the girls, there was no more singing in the fields or music in the evening, no more sitting in the warm darkness to see the stars and hear the wind whispering in the mountains.

One by one, the five boys went away. Pedro and the two youngest had gone to São Paulo, where there was money. Jose and Sebastian had hired themselves out to a big plantation owner in the south. But even with fewer mouths to feed, there was little food. Their father worked less and less in their own fields and scarcely at all for the planter who employed him. Most of his money was spent on drink, and when he wasn't drinking he was sleeping. There was no money for a doctor, and their mother grew weaker, until one day she ceased to cough and fight for breath.

The days and weeks that followed were bleak and desolate. Sometimes their father came home late at night or early in the morning and settled into a drunken sleep. Sometimes he threw Anna a few coins, but no words were exchanged. Maria never spoke or cried. She sometimes stole a piece of bread or a scrap of cheese out of sheer hunger, but her mind was wrapped in clouds as dark as those that hung over the Brazilian mountains—just before the lightning flashed.

Sometimes Anna felt that there would be such a storm, and she knew that she must act before that time came. Gradually it came to her what she must do.

On the way to town, Anna always passed a large house surrounded by trees, a flowering hedge and a white gate. Children played under the trees. Their feet were bare and their clothes shabby, but they were clean, and they laughed and sang and looked well–fed.

Two women also lived there, women with kind faces. Anna often walked this road to stand where she could not be seen and watch the children. At times she saw the women playing with these children and marching with tambourines.

Anna had watched so often that she had begun to recognize the children and realized that new ones were often added to the group. She could tell because at first, they were thin and slow, like Maria and herself; but it was not long before they were playing with the other children, brisk and happy.

What would happen if she and Maria lived in that house and played in that garden? The thought became an obsession.

One morning Anna had taken all the ragged scraps of clothes that belonged to her and Maria, washed them vigorously and laid them in the sunshine to dry. Now she was folding them into a neat bundle.

"Come, Maria," she instructed. "Put this on." Anna held out the clean garment, a simple dress that she called Maria's best. Maria, hearing an urgency in Anna's voice, quickly scrambled into it.

Anna took the grubby little garment that Maria had discarded and one of her own, and threw them on the little cooking fire. "We won't need them again," she said.

Anna then took a broom and began to sweep the rooms. Soon her work was done and, with the bundle of clothes under one arm, she pulled her sister to her feet and walked out the door, closing it carefully behind her. Together, she and Maria walked toward a new life.

Although Anna thought she had been unobserved as she watched the playing children outside the large house, the captain in charge of the Salvation Army Children's Home had seen her often. She had even asked about her in the shops around the town.

"She has a sister, the poor little things," said the old woman who weighs the flour and sugar. "They've had a hard life. Their mother's dead, God rest her soul, and their father—well, he drinks, he doesn't work. There used to be boys in the family, but they've moved on."

So when the captain opened the door to Anna and Maria, she was almost expecting them.

"Can we live here, please?" Anna was polite, remembering her mother's teaching.

"Come in," said the captain, as questions flashed through her mind: Where would she put them? Was there enough money to buy food for two more children? What would their father say? What about the authorities?

The next day, the captain found their father, and by applying some hot coffee, brought him a few moments of sobriety. When he asked Anna what she wanted to do, she was untroubled by the decision, which, in her mind, had already been made.

"I want to stay here," said Anna, "and so does Maria."

Maria said nothing.

The civic authorities, represented by a bored young man in a dust–laden office, were happy to be relieved of responsibilities.

As for space and food—the captain knew that two older children were due to leave, and it was amazing how food could be stretched.

And faith, in times of necessity, often seems to provide the needed money. The captain did not worry, she prayed.

Anna fitted into her new surroundings like a hand into a glove, but Maria was not so happy. She rebelled against everything. Everybody kept talking to her, yet she wouldn't talk. She was urged to play in the sunshine, but by now she had forgotten how to play.

Their clothes, if not new, were clean and not ragged. Their food, if not fancy, was fresh and wholesome. Anna always ate what was put before her and sang and danced and played merrily. But Maria was still like a thundercloud on the Brazilian mountaintop, isolated, waiting to explode in a downpour.

Even with her insight into the minds of children, the captain could scarcely explain the deep wound in Maria's spirit, but she kept loving the child. In spite of every rebuff, every shrug of the shoulder, every down–turned lip from Maria, love was still evident in the touch of the captain's hand, in her smile, in her quiet voice.

"We have a new pet," the captain said one morning at breakfast. Immediately there was a chorus of questions. "What is it? A monkey? A rabbit?"

"No, it's a baby goat. Its mother died. Paulo found them both on the roadside. Now who would like to look after it?"

"Captain, Captain, I will look after it!"

"Can it be mine?"

"Where is it?"

The children were falling over themselves with eagerness. Then the captain's attention was caught by the sight of Maria. The same eagerness of the other children was in her face, the tenseness of her little body was eloquent, but she couldn't express it in words.

"Come, Maria." The captain prayed as she spoke. "The baby goat shall be yours." She held out her hand. Maria's small hand quickly slid into hers. Together, they walked toward the baby goat named Bella.

Then the change in Maria began. The thundercloud that for so long had hung over Maria's spirit was dispersing. Because the orphaned state of the animal matched her own, she could relate to its needs and begin to care for them.

Maria also had to speak because she had to ask for Bella's food. When she gave Bella some milk to drink, she would now drink a cupful for herself. And knowing that Bella was sleeping comfortably made it easier for her to go contentedly to bed when the captain called her.

But there was something more to the change in Maria. She began to recognize love because she felt love for Bella. When that happened, she also began to feel the captain's love for her. The stories she heard in the Home Sunday school, stories about Jesus and God's love, began to make sense.

In the past, she had not understood why the captain loved her. Now she knew why. The captain loved Jesus, the Man who loved everybody, so the captain could love everybody, as well. That was why she could give herself to loving children like her—boys and girls who came to her dirty, lonely, disillusioned. The misfits and the tragic accidents of life.

Maria could not put all this into words, but she recognized love when she saw it like this. So it was an almost expected outcome that one day Maria said to the captain, "I want to be like Jesus."

Dorothy O. Joy

Lost and Found

Worry hung heavy over Booth House. Residents of New York City's Bowery district were oddly quiet, almost passive, which usually meant trouble ahead. Miss Cora, assistant to the major–in–charge of the Salvation Army's hostel for men, fooled herself into thinking it was just the sultry, humid closeness—a prologue to summer storms.

Not so.

Little Isaac should have returned from work long ago. Actually, he wasn't that little or that young unless he was compared to the other Isaac, the security guard on duty.

"Are you sure you remember the directions?" Lou, the room clerk, and the older Isaac had fretted like two mother hens that morning while seeing Little Isaac off for his first day at his first job.

"Oh, I remember," Little Isaac had assured them. Then he had pulled out the map they had drawn in preparation. "You showed me real good yesterday."

"What happens if you lose your subway token?" asked Lou.

"Got two more in my right shoe, and lunch money in the left if I lose my lunch—and my feet hurt."

"Where do you work?" asked Isaac.

Little Isaac enunciated each word carefully. "New York City Park Service and"—anticipating their next question—"and my home's Booth House."

They had shoved him out the door, breathing a prayer as he sprinted down the Bowery. Little Isaac whispered the way to himself as he went: two blocks right, turn right, one block straight, down the stairs, take train on left that says F, go five stops . . .

Booth House's newest and youngest protegé had the mind of a child, the body of a seventeen–year–old and a steadfast belief in everyone's innate goodness. But this had not always been so.

When Little Isaac had first come to Booth House, the elevator had terrified him. He would trudge the eight floors to his cubicle and cower whenever spoken to until he was put on medication to relax him. Simple food–service fare was too rich for his sensitive, malnourished stomach. When Lou had given him a transistor radio, even the noise from that had frightened him. Eventually Little Isaac had learned to trust Lou enough for answers to questions when he finally emerged from his shell.

Little Isaac and the older Isaac had two common denominators—they were black and had the same name. He had never known his legitimate father, so Big Isaac became his. The burly security guard had been overwhelmed at the responsibility, at first, but would have been the last to admit it. Big Isaac's first task had been to teach Little Isaac to trust the other residents, to believe that nobody was going to rip him off.

Now, somewhere out there among the perils of "Fun City," Little Isaac was lost and trying to get back to the safety of his haven, back to friends he had finally learned to trust, a home he had learned to love and a God he had learned to believe in.

Big Isaac and Lou huddled outside the entrance in the oppressive air waiting apprehensively for that familiar gait. Both of them knew that Little Isaac was afraid of storms.

"Where in tarnation could he be?" Lou was a born worry–wart.

"I'm off duty in fifteen minutes. I'll retrace the same run we did yesterday."

"Any sign of him?" Miss Cora joined the two scanning the street. She usually came on strong with something from Proverbs to back her up. For once, she couldn't think of a single one. A clap of thunder made them all jump suddenly.

Lou knew her well enough to laugh. "For once, Somebody up there out–boomed you," he kidded.

When it became obvious that Little Isaac was opening up to the folks at Booth House, Miss Cora had entered the picture wearing determination. Early one morning she came to a full halt in front of a more–than–generous tray of breakfast and the blaring transistor radio.

"Turn that thing down," she boomed. He obeyed. "Here's another present," thrusting a package in his hands. "I just about tore New York apart finding the right one." It was a new, beautifully illustrated Bible.

"Well, Isaac?" Lou, sitting next to him, prodded dutifully.

"Thank you, Miss Cora." Isaac fingered the Book gingerly. "I can't read, but I'll sure study the pictures."

"That's the spirit!" She gave him a motherly hug. "Don't thank me; thank Him." Then she buzzed off.

Several more residents now emerged to join the trio standing vigil outside the hotel. Lightning had joined the thunder.

"Looks more like midnight than four o'clock," observed one.

"That puts the young man four hours overdue," said another.

A third was pessimistic. "Maybe he split for good."

"He wouldn't know how." Lou was indignant. "This is the only home he ever had."

With one more thunderous clap, the sky opened up. Miss Cora, muttering something about summer flu epidemics, shooed everyone back through the door. Lou worried inside—they had forgotten to give him a raincoat.

Little Isaac and his two gifts, his radio and his Bible, had become inseparable. He spent hours explaining his Bible's pictures to blind old Mr. Foster, who sat all day in the lobby of Booth House by the security office. He, too, had a radio, and it was a toss–up as to which blared louder. Mr. Foster knew Bible history so well he needed no eyes to explain it. In between baseball games on the radio, he revealed each story to the enthralled young convert.

Big Isaac and Lou had split the money to buy their charge a new outfit for Friday night church at 14th Street. Little Isaac, being very fond of his suit, was always ready two hours early for the bus so he could preen around in the lobby.

The major emerged from his office to assess the situation. He motioned to Big Isaac whose shift was just ending. "I'll drive you to the train station. Maybe he's there waiting for the storm to finish."

Just then, the door burst open and there stood Little Isaac with a grin from ear to ear, soaked to the skin and clutching his Bible.

"I'm back!" His shout soared over the storm. "It's me, Isaac. Remember me? I'm back." Behind him stood a familiar black bonnet and a rain cape with the trim of lieutenant. Little Isaac grabbed her hand and propelled her forward eagerly to meet his "family."

Miss Cora was so overcome she almost smothered him. Lou and Big Isaac had the same urge but refrained. They settled for a hearty handshake. And then the facts unfolded.

Because of storm warnings, the Park Service had finished early at the *opposite end* of Central Park. Little Isaac had wandered around—hopelessly lost—until, a miracle! He spotted the lieutenant talking to a group of children and recognized her uniform from Friday church services. She, too, was carrying a familiar book—His Word.

He hung around the fringes of the group until the lieutenant smiled at him. "That sure is a pretty Bible you have, young man." She had noticed his Bible, which he always carried with him. He showed it to her eagerly. She recognized Miss Cora's signature in the inscription and knew the address. Little Isaac had found an escort home.

"I guess this calls for a celebration." Miss Cora turned to Lou and Big Isaac. "You two, see what the men in food service can whip up fast that's special." Then she wiped the rain from Little Isaac's face. "How would you like two jobs instead of one?" Little Isaac looked at her quizzically. "We'll open a Lost and Found department at Booth House, and I think Little Isaac is qualified for the job in more ways than one."

They all laughed, including Little Isaac. He wasn't quite sure he understood, but he knew it had to be all right because he was home.

Maurice E. Pollom

New Station Superintendent

Lance McAllister was enjoying a cup of coffee in the swing room of the postal station where he worked when the superintendent, Gene Farris, walked by.

"Stop by my desk before you start work," Farris said. "Got something to tell you."

Lance finished his coffee, then walked over to Gene's desk.

"Sit down, sit down," said Gene. "I just wanted to tell you that I'm retiring at the end of this month."

"You are!"

"Yes, and I hope you apply for the job. I was in the postmaster's office yesterday filling out the retirement form when I suggested that you should be the man to take my place. I told Evans that you had a growing family, and you need the extra income. Plus, I said you're well–qualified. He said you should fill out an application. So, if you want the job, pal, you'd better apply."

"Well, this is a surprise," said Lance. "I don't know what to say. You're really retiring?"

"That's right, my friend. After thirty–five years, I think it's time."

"If you're going to retire, I would like the job. But do you think I have a chance?"

"I don't know. There may be others in line, but you'll never know unless you try."

Lance thought for a moment, then said, "Do you suppose I could take a couple of hours annual leave tomorrow morning? I'll go down and apply first thing."

"Sure, that can be arranged." Gene smiled as he nodded.

The next morning Lance drove to the main office, application at the ready, to see the postmaster.

"Hello, Miss Carty," he greeted the postmaster's secretary.

"Why, hello, Lance," she replied. "Haven't seen you for some time."

"Been about a year, I guess," said Lance. "Is Mr. Evans in?"

"Yes." She pushed a button to announce Lance's arrival.

"Hello, McAllister," the postmaster greeted him from behind his desk after Lance had been announced. "Bet I know why you're here."

"You probably do, sir. Gene Farris told me yesterday he is retiring at the end of the month. I'd like to apply for the station superintendent job. I've already filled out an application." He fished into his inside coat pocket and placed the application on the desk.

The postmaster paused. "When the word gets out that Gene is retiring, I'll be expecting quite a few applications. That's a pretty good job out there."

"I know it is, sir. I've been the assistant superintendent for three years now. It's a good place to work. And Gene has been a first–rate boss."

"I'll take your application, McAllister." Mr. Evans cleared his throat. "Of course, there are a lot of factors to consider."

"I'm familiar with the work," said Lance confidently. "I've filled in for Gene quite a few times. I think I could do a good job."

"Do you *think,* or do you *know?*" The postmaster gave Lance an intimidating stare, then said as he rose from his chair, "Being the superintendent involves more than just filling in from time to time, but we'll see, we'll see."

Lance was walked to the door dismissively. He left the office feeling slighted by the postmaster's words—they weren't exactly words of encouragement.

As expected, news of Farris's impending retirement spread fast throughout the station. One morning Lance overheard several carriers talking about who might be the new superintendent.

"You know," said one, "Evans has his buddies. He'll appoint one of them to the job."

"Sure, he can appoint anybody he wants to—qualified or not," said another.

Lance shuddered. The comment about the postmaster's buddies had shaken him. He remembered the time Mr. Evans had hosted a Christmas dinner for all the supervisors and had ordered drinks. When Lance had respectfully declined the cocktail, Mr. Evans had made a disparaging comment about "those who refuse to have a social drink with their friends."

Although Lance felt he didn't have much of a chance, when he prayed that night, he asked God to help him get the appointment as station superintendent. He promised the Lord also that if he didn't get the job, he would cooperate with his new boss.

The next morning when Lance walked into the station, it was unusually quiet. He went to the bulletin board and saw the announcement: *Effective July 1, Marshall Rogers is appointed Station Superintendent at Eastside Station, replacing Eugene Farris, retiring June 30.*

Marshall Rogers? Marshall Rogers, who had been appointed postal clerk only ten years ago, had learned window clerk duties at Eastside Station—and Lance had been the one to train him! Marshall had risen rapidly through the ranks and was now an assistant superintendent in the finance section of the main post office. To think that a much younger man—someone he himself had trained—would now be his supervisor was almost more than Lance could bear.

Lance fumed: *Well, if the postmaster thinks Marshall Rogers is such a good man, he won't need me to help him! If I'm not good enough for the job, I certainly am not good enough to teach someone else how to do the work. It just isn't fair! I have over twenty years of service here. It's not right that I'll be working for a man who's put in half the time I have.*

The last week of June was miserable for Lance. And then, on the day before the new superintendent was to start, Marshall Rogers phoned Lance and wanted to know if he could come and talk to Lance at his home after work that evening. Even as Lance answered, "Sure, come on out," he wondered why Marshall wanted to see him.

"Hello, Lance," Marshall greeted him at the door that night.

"Come on in," said Lance unenthusiastically.

"I wanted to talk to you about the superintendent's job before I take over tomorrow," said Marshall.

They sat in the living room, and Marshall fidgeted in his chair.

"This isn't easy," Marshall began, "Evans told me you applied for the job, too, and I remember you were the one who taught me the ropes at Eastside Station."

Lance didn't answer.

"I just want you to know I have mixed feelings about this. The main reason I applied for the job is because I wanted to work at a station that's closer to home. Besides, I want to get away from the main office."

"I can understand that," said Lance.

"You know," said Marshall, "everyone tells me you're a Christian. I used to be one myself." He paused, then continued ruefully, "But then I began socializing with the guys, thinking it would help me in my career. You know . . . the drinking, the night clubs, all that. I'd like to think that, by transferring out here, I can get away from that stuff. I want to get back into church—back to the Lord."

Lance stared at Marshall doubtfully, but then he remembered his prayer. He had promised the Lord he would cooperate with the new superintendent. What better way than to witness to Marshall?

Lance softened. "I will help you in any way I can," he said.

Marshall looked genuinely grateful.

Lance thought a moment, then said, "Maybe we could start by praying together right now."

Crane Delbert Bennett

A Swedish Saga

Captain Ellen Elisabeth Blomkvist finished packing her trunks. At long last! The time had come and she was about to realize her heart's longtime yearning, to be a missionary to the Lapps!

A faithful officer in The Salvation Army in Sweden, Ellen had promised to serve the Lord all the days of her life. Then the telegram arrived from headquarters informing her that she was to leave for America, not Lappland!

America! How could the Lord use her there, she wondered. She could neither speak, write nor read English! She knew that the Army had recently opened a branch of their work in the Swedish language in America and that the many Scandinavian immigrants streaming into the country needed the gospel. Swedes, Norwegians, Danes and Finns had left their native countries and spread out over America late in the century to begin new lives in towns and cities they built. By the end of 1889 over 400,000 Scandinavians had come to the new land, bringing with them their Christian faith, their love for the Bible and their commitment to a personal God.

Captain Blomkvist was stunned by the telegram, but she fell down on her knees and asked God for guidance. If God wanted her to go to America, then she would go.

Ellen received her farewell orders from General William Booth, founder of The Salvation Army, along with three other Swedish officers. Staff–Captain Hildur Karlson was also to sail to America, and two male officers were assigned to Germany. The four officers marched two–by–two onto the platform, Staff–Captain Karlson and Captain Blomkvist carrying the Stars and Stripes flag of America, and the two men with wide bands across their chests, symbolic of the German flag.

With the memory of Colonel Lawley's prayer and the warm hand-clasp of William Booth to comfort her, Captain Blomkvist and Staff–Captain Karlson set sail for America on February 11, 1897.

The ship docked in New York City after a rough voyage, and the two pairs of eyes scanned the crowds anxiously for the well–known Salvation Army uniform, but no one was there to meet them. When they arrived at the headquarters address, they found to their dismay that the doors were locked!

Ellen rang the bell persistently until a man appeared.

"No one here!" he shouted through the closed door.

Staff–Captain Karlson knocked harder in response. "Ve just come from England—ve have no place to go!"

The nightwatchman stared at them and at their baggage, thought for a moment, then opened the door. "The offices are closed, no one here. But come in."

"Can—can ve stay overnight?" Staff–Captain Karlson explained their plight, but the watchman told them there were no rooms for sleeping. After a pause, he led them to a room with some wooden benches and a nearby restroom, where they could wash.

The two officers stood looking at each other, then burst out laughing! It did not matter that no one had been there to greet them—they had reached Salvation Army headquarters in America, and it was a beginning of a new phase in their service to God and the Army!

While nibbling some fruit, biscuits and candy left from their trip, they knelt down and thanked God for a safe crossing.

On March 1, 1897, Lt. Colonel Richard Holz, then commander of the Scandinavian work in America, welcomed them warmly and gave them orders to travel with him and a few other officers to New England, where they would conduct special meetings.

While at Quincy, Massachusetts, during the evening meeting, Ellen spotted a familiar face in the audience—her sister Esther, who had left Sweden a few years before! Ellen could hardly sit still on the platform! She wanted to rush down and put her arms around her sister. When the meeting was over, the two sisters had a jubilant reunion.

After Brockton, the Salvationists went to Boston and Lynn and held meetings there, where many souls were won for God. Staff–Captain Karlson was then asked to travel to the north–central states and help the work there, while Captain Ellen Blomkvist received orders to take command of Brooklyn No. 3, the first Swedish corps in Brooklyn, New York. She went obediently but often recalled her native Sweden and marveled at the mysterious ways of the Lord.

Ellen remembered the first time she had met The Salvation Army in Nässjö, Sweden—where she had grown up with one sister and two brothers. As a small child, her father had often taken her to the railroad station to watch the trains come and go. So it was natural for her, when called as a teenager to tell others about Christ, to choose the railroad station in Nässjö to do her witnessing for the Lord.

Ellen would take her guitar to the station, sit on a bench where the travellers waited for their trains, and sing gospel songs.

One day a prominent businessman from Stockholm made it a point to learn her name and who she was before he boarded his train. This same businessman was a good friend of Commissioner Hannah Ouchterlony, the commander–in–chief of the Salvation Army work in Sweden. "You must find that young girl next time you are in Nässjö. She is a born Salvationist!" he had told Ouchterlony.

The commissioner had promised to look up the girl. But before Ellen Blomkvist met Commissioner Ouchterlony, she spent that same summer in Mosseberg, Sweden, with her aunt, the head baker in a prominent hotel there. It was while she was there, learning the baker's trade, that The Salvation Army sent a brigade of Salvationists to Mosseberg with the hope of opening a corps. Until then, Ellen had known nothing about the Army and its work, but she went to the meetings out of sheer curiosity.

Amazed and wide–eyed, Ellen listened to the Salvationists sing and play. The leader of the group was Captain James Toft (later Commissioner Toft, missionary and leader of Salvation Army work in many countries). When the testimonies began, something tugged at her heart! She loved Jesus, too, and wanted to tell the world about

Him just as the Salvationists were doing. At the close of the last meeting, Ellen was the first to go forward and make her commitment to God. The date was June 15, 1887.

When the summer ended, Ellen went home to Nässjö to continue learning about the Salvationists, who had stirred her interest. As the Army's weekly paper, *Stridsropet* (*War Cry*), began arriving at the Blomkvist home, Ellen and her parents liked what they read. When Ellen said that there ought to be a corps in Nässjö, her father agreed.

Sven Blomkvist wrote to the Army's headquarters in Stockholm. It wasn't long before Captain Lindblad and a brigade of Salvationists arrived in Nässjö to start the work.

Ellen and her father went early to the railroad station to welcome the Salvationists led by Captain Lindblad, who was a young girl not much older than Ellen. The meetings were held in a small church, where Captain Lindblad proved herself an able preacher!

A few weeks later Commissioner Ouchterlony visited with Ellen, on the suggestion of the Stockholm businessman, and asked her to sing and play her guitar. Deeply touched by Ellen's youthful exuberance and talent, the commissioner placed her hands on Ellen's shoulders. "Would you like to walk in the Master's footsteps, telling the world about Him, saving the sinful, rescuing the fallen, finding the lost with us in The Salvation Army?"

Ellen was stunned! She wanted to work for Jesus—and The Salvation Army wanted her! Commissioner Ouchterlony smiled. "Think it over, my dear, and then let me know."

That had been the beginning.

In America, Ellen married Carl August Bergh, a young Swedish officer who served at a New York City hotel for homeless men. After their marriage in 1899, Captain and Mrs. Carl Bergh served as officers of the Swedish corps in Jamestown, New York, and later Duluth, Minnesota.

A gifted writer, Ellen wrote more than one hundred poems and songs, plus many articles that were published in the *Stridsropet,* both in America and abroad. One of those songs began on a cold morning in Duluth when a hurdy-gurdy cranked out a delightful melody that captured Ellen's attention. She went to the window to listen. It was a popular song of that day, "The Banks of the Wabash." She asked the man to play the song again and again. Picking out the melody on the piano, she soon had the notes on paper. The words flowed from her pen, and *"Buren Utav Nädens Vind"* ("Carried by the Wind of Grace") was born! The popular song is included in every Scandinavian Salvation Army *Song Book* in Europe and America.

Years later Major Kaleb Johnson wrote the English translation:

Carried by the wind of Grace my thoughts are lifted
To the mountain top of glory bright and fair,
Where a glimpse of heav'n I see when clouds are rifted,
And I hear the strains of songs of victory there.

I behold, by faith, the matchless heavenly portals
And the glory of the open pearly gates,
Oh, what boundless joy and pleasure for us mortals
In that wondrous land of promise now awaits.

Like a "golden sunrise" on a summer morning
Spreads across the eastern sky so bright and fair,
So the saints, the beauty of the Lord adorning,
Now are coming home to God from everywhere!

Ellen became one of the foremost speakers in the Scandinavian Department. She led meetings and campaigns during the twenty-six years in which her husband served as the editor of *Stridsropet* in New York. After his death, she continued her public ministry until she was called home on December 1, 1932.

Ellen Blomkvist Bergh was a true Army pioneer, a great lady, wife and mother. I know because she was my beloved mother!

Brita Wicklund

To Live Again

Joe Brennan shifted the songbook to the other hand and cleared his throat. The music was cheerful, inspiring even, but his voice did not complement it. Rather, his raspy, quavering bass seemed a mockery.

Why couldn't he sing anymore? Once he had been a member of the songster brigade. He'd taken it for granted then, even complained a time or two when a practice took up too much time. Well, the truth was, his singing days were over. He knew it.

Since the operation, there just wasn't much he could do. The doctor said he had come through it in great style; if he was careful and did all the right things, his heart would stand him in good stead through his golden years. Joe frowned into the songbook. *Doing what?* he wondered.

He'd had to curtail a lot of activities including the band and songsters. His Sunday school class had retired him with genuine tears and a gold watch. He had known it was best. Still he felt every cold, hard sliver of the shelf on which he'd been placed.

Joe shook himself mentally. What a way to feel on the Lord's Day! God had been good to him. He had used him and blessed him in so many ways. He really wanted to praise the Lord. Still . . .

The song service ended, and the captain was reading the Scripture. Joe opened his worn Bible eagerly. How he needed something special today!

A soft rustle in the aisle drew his attention. A woman sat down in the pew opposite him, smoothing the pink folds of her summery dress with deft young hands. The face that turned upward toward the captain was unusually attractive. Her eyes were dark, and the auburn hair that curled gently about her face shone with good health. That would have been enough to cause Joe to look twice. But there was something more that drew his attention.

He peered at her sidelong over the wire frames of his glasses. The corners of her mouth were rigid, as though they had not smiled for a long time. Lines of worry were there, too, etched incongruously across the expanse of her forehead.

Joe watched her work her fingers back and forth over the handle of her purse. Something in Joe reached out in sympathy to the young woman. He could hardly wait until the end of the meeting. Someone must welcome her. Likely the captain would be busy shaking hands with everyone. This stranger needed a friendly word, and Joe was determined to give it—well, at least he could do that.

She would have walked right on by, but Joe stretched out his big hand. "I'm Joe Brennan. So nice to have you here today."

The smile she gave him was brief but warm, unlike her hand that was incredibly cold for a hot Texas day. "Thank you," she said in a soft voice that showed her weariness. She took a step toward the door.

Joe took a step, too. "Do you live in town, ma'am?" he asked, hoping he didn't sound too nosy.

"No, I'm just visiting. I—" She looked nervously down, then turned her brown eyes again to him. "My name is Marcia Jenner. I'm from Virginia. My son and I are here for a while. You see, he's going to have surgery here."

Joe was afraid for a moment that she was going to cry or something. He wished he were better at this kind of thing, but actually he'd always been a pensive sort. "Oh, I see."

He thought he said all the right things about praying for the boy and hoping that everything would turn out well. But the words seemed lifeless and inadequate.

Joe introduced her to the captain, who greeted her warmly enough. But he was immediately snagged by Mrs. Haggerty, who always had some pressing problem or other to discuss with him. Joe watched the woman step out into the afternoon light. Depressed, he made a mental note of her name.

During his talk with Mrs. Jenner, Joe had learned that she was a former Salvationist. He wondered what had brought about the separation and how things stood with her and the Lord. Well, surely the captain would get up to see her and the boy that week. Joe hurried to catch up with his wife, waiting for him at the door.

As the day wore on, Joe felt more tired and useless than he had in months. The ball game was boring, and his afternoon nap eluded him. His mind kept returning to Mrs. Jenner.

How frightening to be in a strange city, facing what was obviously a serious surgery. Worse yet, Mrs. Jenner didn't seem strong enough in the way a person needed to be strong in times of stress. What would he ever have done, he wondered, without the Lord, without the knowledge of His love and care, during his own ordeal?

"Okay, Lord, I get the message," Joe said into the mirror. He pulled his Salvation Army uniform tunic over his broad chest, frowning a little at the protrusion just below it.

The hospital corridors were cold, and though people were all about, he felt a penetrating loneliness. Poor Mrs. Jenner. Hospitals were bad enough, but away from loved ones and friends, it must seem unbearable. Joe quickened his steps, hardly noticing that he was short of breath.

He found Mrs. Jenner and the boy in a small, private room. She rose from her chair by the bed when he came in. Joe thought her tired eyes brightened, though her smile was slow in coming.

"Hello, Mrs. Jenner," he said, taking the hand she offered.

"How kind of you to come, Mr. Brennan." She stepped closer to the bed. "This is my son, Keith."

Joe looked into the face of a child about ten. Dark hair like his mother's shrouded his pale face. He looked much too small for the enormous white bed. Joe felt a lump spring up in his throat.

Keith's eyes were hopeful. "Hello," he said. He looked from Joe to his mother awkwardly.

"Mr. Brennan is from The Salvation Army, Keith. He has come to visit you."

Joe liked the boy instantly. "You know, I have a grandson about your age, Keith."

It was easy to talk to Keith. Joe found himself enjoying the visit immensely. He couldn't help feeling sorry for the boy, though. His life had been full of sickness, and now he was facing a major operation.

"Keith, I believe that God loves you very much and that He is watching over you. Is it okay if I pray with you before I leave?" Joe smiled reassuringly with a quick glance at the boy's mother.

Joe finished the prayer and promised to return the next day. Keith Jenner seemed pleased. "See ya," he said with a smile.

Marcia Jenner stepped into the hall with Joe. He saw that her eyes were glistening with tears.

Joe cleared his throat. "I hope you don't mind. I mean—" He clasped Mrs. Jenner's hand, not knowing what to say.

"No, Mr. Brennan, I don't mind. I'm very grateful." She paused and dabbed her nose with her handkerchief. "You see, I—I have been bitter and confused for some time now. I guess I was mad at God, or something. I don't know. It seems kind of senseless, when you put it into words. But—you've helped me realize that I was turning away from the very One who could help us." A soft light appeared in her dark eyes. "I just want to thank you for your prayers and—well, for being so kind to us."

Joe felt his feet barely touching ground as he walked down the corridor. He glanced at his gold watch. Really, it was quite a nice watch at that. And if he hurried he'd have time to check on Mrs. Watson. He had heard she was in the hospital for tests. She probably needed a friend, too.

Joe quickened his steps. He hadn't felt so young in years!

Lt. Colonel Marlene Chase

How Luk Became a Christian

Luk sat at the table, papers spread before him. His fine pen was poised to complete the final part of his candidate's papers. His careful writing, having the delicacy of his native Chinese characters, already filled many lines. No blot or erasure spoiled his meticulous work.

Luk's complete absorption in his work and his thoughts made him impervious to the flood of sound below him on the streets. Traffic whirled and grated—ancient Chinese carts vying for space with sleek American cars, air–conditioned against the Hong Kong summer heat. There was incessant noise, in fact, in the huge apartment block where—in tiny rooms like this one—three thousand men, women and children slept, ate, quarreled, made love, died—happy or miserable, according to their natures.

Luk's brother Wang bent his head studiously over his book. His mother moved silently around the stove, preparing rice for the evening meal. His father stitched at the work he had brought from the shop, his needle whipping in and out of the soft, bright material. Tomorrow this piece of clothing would be bought by a tourist, who would go home—to Kansas City or Seattle or Boston—and boast of how she had bargained with a little Chinese tailor in Hong Kong.

It had not always been like this.

Luk's thoughts drifted as far back as he could remember. The years unrolled like a panorama. He was no longer in the room in the Resettlement Block but in the little hut his father had built in the hills of Kwai Chung. He knew nothing else, no other home.

It was early morning, and the sun was already hot on the stony slopes. The ramshackle huts huddled against each other as if seeking support should the hurricane season come.

Luk's mother was hurrying to her daily work as an *ayah* in Kowloon, and his father had started off for the city before sunup.

"I don't want to go for water today," Luk was saying sullenly. His bare toes twisted in the worn earth. "Let Wang go." Then he shouted for his brother. "Wang!"

His mother laughed gently, almost soundlessly. "He's too small, not strong and brave as you are."

She looked confidently at her eight–year–old child. She knew Luk would go, for this was a daily trial. Always there was the same protest, but every day he took his place in the struggling, jostling queue at the standpipe at the bottom of the hill. Luk would be pushed and kicked in the fight for position, and then shoved playfully as he labored with his slopping pail back up the rocky path. But each day he managed to bring enough water for the family needs—for cooking rice, for the thick, vegetable soup and the pale brown tea. The washing of clothes, faces, hands, dusty feet was done in the little stream that curled round the base of the hill.

The hut was empty when Luk returned with the water. Wang was playing in the dust outside. That whole hot day they played together on the hillside, scuffled with one another, cooled their feet in the little stream, went back to the hut for a handful of cold rice, and fell asleep in the shade of a rustling tree.

Luk awoke to the sound of voices. He ran to the house and then stopped as he saw his father's angry face. The paper–thin walls—so thin that at night Luk could hear the snores of Ho Ling whose hut abutted theirs—shook as his father paced rapidly from one wall to the other. "I will not go." He struck his fist on the table.

"They could make you," came the diffident response from his mother.

"Make me! No one can do that—not even the government with its story of 'wanting a better life for everybody' and its polite notices." He crumpled the piece of paper he was carrying.

"There will be water streaming from a tap, and light from a wall switch, honorable husband."

"I will not live in a man–made mountain," his father said, stamping his foot.

"I could do laundry work for the rich Americans." His mother's voice was hesitant but persuasive.

"I will not live in an ant hill with three thousand other ants." Luk's father threw the official notice on the floor, sat down heavily and went on with his sewing.

"Esteemed husband, Luk and Wang could go to school, perhaps." Gentle Shan knew how to deploy her arguments.

"They shall not learn about a foreign god," he muttered.

"There will be no god teaching. It will be a government school."

"Silence, wife." His father went on stitching, his mind weaving thoughts as rapidly as his needle dove in and out through the silk.

He weighed the advantages of the move against the one principle disadvantage in his mind of losing his free will. There would be the water, the light, more money and the school—maybe. It was a hard decision to make, but he supposed he might as well accept the change without any more fuss. The government would keep its word and demolish all these huts. Then they would become vagrants and have nothing at all. He took the bowl of rice his wife handed him and said defiantly, "It is not right, but we will go."

In Luk's mind, it seemed like the next day, but it would have been a month later when they piled their belongings into a borrowed cart and trundled into the city.

Bed rolls, the little stove, their meager toys, the few clothes they kept against the winter cold—it was no great chore to dispose of the entire contents in the room allotted them in the vast Resettlement Block in Tai Wo Hau. Nor did it take Luk long to explore and report on his exciting surroundings. Thousands of people lived all around them! There were stores and a playground—and a school!

"There is a school, honored Father."

"That is known."

"It is the Kwong Yueh School of The Salvation Army. It is on the rooftop. I could go easily."

Luk was not discouraged by his father's disapproving silence.

"You will not go," said his father finally. "I have said there shall be no god teaching. That is the end."

"Chen Lui's sons go to a rooftop school, esteemed husband." Shan's dark head was bent submissively over her ironing.

"He will let his sons go anywhere so that he is not troubled. He has no thought for the spirit of his ancestors."

"It is said his sons are clever, more so than the other boys in the school." Shan was willing to use any weapon in defense of her sons.

"Who is Chen Lui that he should have sons more clever than any others? The sons of my honored wife would let none step before them on the ladder of learning." He was silent for a moment. "But they shall have no god teaching."

"No one will ever know the cleverness of our sons. It will remain as hidden treasure forever. They will be mere porters or gardeners— nothing that requires school learning." Then Shan continued with slight disparagement in her voice, "Of course, you could teach them to use a needle, I suppose."

Luk, playing in his corner with tins and string, shivered. To sit all day stitching! He would not do it.

"Honored parent," he stood politely before his father, "I need not remember what the teacher says about her religion."

The father looked speculatively at the small figure in the shabby shirt. Maybe his wife was right. He should not withhold education from these children and condemn them to a life of slavery such as his.

"If that can be so, and you do not forego the religion of your ancestors, then I will ask if you may be a student."

So, Luk went daily to school, high above the city. He proudly wore his school uniform with the emblem of The Salvation Army, the clear, bright red shield, on his blazer just above his heart. (Not yet in his heart, though that would come one day.)

Soon a big problem presented itself: Daily the teacher would read from the Christian's holy book, and try as he would, Luk was not able to forget the words he heard. He struggled to keep his promise to his father, but the stories he heard—about a Man who came from the Great One Himself—were lodging in his heart as well as his mind. Luk could understand these stories, for they were so simple, telling about a man sowing corn or fishermen with their nets, such as he could see every day. There was even a little joke about a tailor who knew it was wrong to sew new cloth into an old garment. He had told his father that tale, and his father agreed that the man spoke truth.

That was what Luk wanted, the truth—about himself, about the world, about why people were poor and hungry, about that part in him which longed for goodness, about a god who was always near. The Christian God was not an ancestor sitting on a shelf but Someone who was with him all the time, interested in him, Luk. That was what he longed for.

Luk observed his teacher, that calm, small person. Happiness shone from her brown eyes and a smile often creased her smooth pale cheeks. Even when she was cross—and that was inevitable with a class of fifty small children—her voice was never too loud. He knew that she went to Salvation Army meetings, managed the Sunday school, wore a Salvation Army hat. What he did not yet know was the power of God in a person's life or the unremitting care of a devoted missionary in a children's home.

But he also knew that, above all else, he wanted to be like her.

"Teacher," he said one day, "can I come to your school on Sunday?"

Teacher looked at him thoughtfully. "What will your father say?"

"He need not know." As he spoke, Luk felt that would be wrong.

"He must know because my school is not like a rooftop school. It is a place where we talk about God and the Man Jesus. That will not please your father, Luk."

"I do not think he will mind, respected teacher. He has been to the end of term exercises, and he thinks your singing is good and that the words of your big Man are very wise. He cannot understand why everyone who thinks as you do is so happy, even when you are poor and live as we do."

The two years in which Luk had been learning in the rooftop

school had changed his father's ideas drastically. He was not himself ready to throw over all he believed, but the sincerity and earnestness of the teacher and her employers had disturbed the foundations of his thinking. He had looked at the thousands of children who went to the Salvation Army schools and who sang at the end of term exercises. He had listened to the young people speaking in street meetings.

"You may go," his father said to Luk, "but you must become like your teacher." There was a mysterious sadness in his heart. Perhaps he knew that his son would follow a different path than his own.

Luk blossomed like a flower in the sunshine. He absorbed the Christian teaching as eagerly as he had taken in facts at the rooftop school. And then came the day when another teacher asked, "When will you make a decision for Christ?"

"That is what I must do," he replied. "I will accept this God who is always near, this Person who comes into a man's heart, this Spirit which can change everything in one, even though the world outside is still the same."

With a start the eighteen–year–old Luk stopped his daydreaming. He was back in his room again, high above the city streets, his mother still cooking, his father stitching, Wang reading. Everything was still the same—and yet not the same.

So that is the story of how Luk came to be sitting, pen in hand, completing his candidate's papers and trying to put into his best English the facts of how he came to be a Christian and a Salvationist, and why he wanted to become an officer of The Salvation Army.

But where did the story really begin? Not with Luk's insistence that he should go to the rooftop school. Not even with the notice from the government arriving to that paper–thin hut on the hills of Kwai Chung. Maybe it began with a prayer in a small Salvation Army corps back home or with a Self–Denial gift. Perhaps you had a share in it.

Dorothy O. Joy

Only Crumbs

I knew Justa was at my door in Galilee when I heard the three quick taps followed by two slower ones. It was our secret code. As soon as I answered her knock, the aura of excitement that enveloped her drew me into its circle.

"Can you keep Bernice today?" she inquired in a staccato–like voice quite unnatural for her. There was a strange gleam in her eyes, and her cheeks glowed as she paced back and forth on my doorstep.

"Of course I will, Justa," I replied, sensing my best friend's urgency. "But won't you have a cup of herb tea first?" I invited her in, knowing her weakness for the hot drink, brewed with choice herbs I gather carefully from their hiding places on the surrounding hillsides. My curiosity was aroused further by her refusal.

"Whatever takes you out so early in the day that you don't have time to share my hospitality along with your favorite tea?" I asked in ill–concealed wonder. The color in her cheeks heightened as she mumbled something about an unexpected errand—a traveling healer, I thought she said. Sensing her uneasiness and secrecy, I stopped my questioning.

Justa and I had been neighbors and bosom companions for twenty years; although we shared many secrets, we respected each other's privacy. I remember when Justa, a youthful bride of fourteen, first moved into the roomy stone house next door—a mansion next to my one–room adobe. How many times she had come to me for advice on cooking, on understanding her husband, and on the best time for planting her garden. Then there were the ten childless years of shame and disgrace when she was openly shunned by the village women because she did not bear children.

Lemuel, her easy–going, good–natured husband, was not bothered by the loose talk. He shrugged his shoulders in indifference whenever the village gossip mistakenly fell on his ears.

"Our lives are complete," he told Justa lovingly. "Nothing will ever mar our happiness so long as we have each other."

The day she learned she was pregnant, Justa was beaming with pride and joy. "At last, the goddess Ashtaroth has absolved me, and I am to bear Lemuel's child," she had exulted with a radiant face. As Justa's date drew near, the anticipation of the happy couple grew along with the precious life within her.

Bernice was a pretty baby blessed with unusual intelligence. Lemuel did not mind that their first–born was a girl, instead of the boy that most fathers hoped for. He was content; Justa had borne his child.

Then, as time went by, the dimpled smile, which won the hearts of all who saw Bernice, was replaced with a snarl—like that of an animal being stalked by hunters. The child's gaze became wild and glassy.

I could see the fear that Justa tried to conceal when her baby was not walking by the time she was eighteen months old. Lemuel, a man of some wealth, spared no money for the best physicians in the land. Justa visited the temple daily, where she offered lavish gifts to all the gods sitting cold and rigid on their marble pedestals. But both gods and physicians failed to alleviate the misery that settled, like a fore-boding cloud, over the erstwhile happy home.

Bernice was two years old before she could even stand on wobbly legs. Slowly she learned to take a few faltering steps. Justa confided in me one day that the fire in their courtyard held a strange attraction for her little one. My troubled thoughts echoed her own. Every time I heard the coarse, guttural voice of the child, instead of sweet baby talk, the hovering horror of suspicion deepened. I sincerely hoped that I was mistaken.

I never will be able to erase the memory of that day when I first heard the frantic screams coming from Bernice next door. A cold, hard terror had gripped Justa as she stood frozen in the courtyard, watching as her child writhed upon the hard–packed earth where she had thrown herself into the smouldering embers of the fire. Bernice had somehow rolled out by herself, thereby smothering the flames that could have snuffed out her feeble life. Justa then uttered a sharp cry and rushed to the frail child—the dearest treasure she had on earth. I knew then that my worst fears were confirmed—Bernice was demon possessed!

The wild, unearthly screams continued to erupt when the demons, in spite of Justa's vigilance, would assault Bernice and throw her mercilessly, repeatedly into the fire. Months could sometimes pass quietly without such onslaughts until I would begin to think that the attacks perhaps had ceased and that the gods had been appeased by Justa's faithful offerings.

Then, without warning, the demons would pounce upon the dear child in all their fury.

Sometimes the demons would cause Bernice to tear her clothes to shreds or to scratch at her own body, leaving long, terrible claw–like marks. The scratches and burns turned into hideous, open sores. Her once–beautiful face with the dimpled smile became, like her entire body, a mass of grotesque scars.

By the time Bernice reached twelve years of age, her stunted growth and scarred body made her look like a wizened old lady. Justa became a mere shadow of the robust bride I used to know, as she cared untiringly for her daughter with a mother's love, ready to try any cure that might heal her troubled daughter.

Then came that unforgettable day when Justa, slightly breathless and headdress askew, knocked on my door and, refusing to stay for tea, thrust the sleeping Bernice in my arms. Determination marked her every step as she turned and sped along the narrow street leading to the edge of town.

How was I to know that when she had gone to the village well to draw water the evening before, she had met Simone, the wife of Clementine, the potter? Simone had been complaining because of the extra water she was forced to draw to accommodate the guests her husband had brought home unexpectedly.

"A Jewish man named Jesus has come," Simone explained, "with some of his students, to seek seclusion. He is a famous healer, Justa, with extraordinary success! In fact, so many come to him to be healed that he found it necessary to bring some of his students here to be assured of uninterrupted peace and quiet so that he could instruct them in his work.

"I heard his students talking about some of the healings their teacher has performed," Simone added confidentially, giving a knowing nod to the now very interested Justa. "He even has the ability to cast out demons."

That night, Justa lay awake listening to her wildly beating heart long after her husband and daughter had fallen asleep. She quietly stepped into the soft shadows of the darkened courtyard to be alone with her thoughts. The silvery moon slipped out from behind the clouds, as though to light her path and breathe a holy benediction upon her weary soul.

I watched Bernice closely that next morning. The demons had been attacking her viciously throughout the week. Usually Justa would not have left her with anyone, not even me, when her child was having these spells. I let the fire in my courtyard die down that day, and we ate only fresh fruit and some bread I had baked the day before. In spite of my efforts to control and protect the child, she tore her cloak several times. I was especially concerned with several of the open sores, which were fiery red. I found some rue among my medicinal herbs and made a poultice, hoping to draw out some of the infection.

It was late afternoon when I heard a soft, musical voice speaking. Startled, I turned to see who had come into the house without my knowledge. No one was there except Bernice. As I came closer to her, a dimpled smile spread across her beautiful face. Her clear eyes sparkled intelligently. In a gentle, melodious voice she asked, "Will you come home with me to find a tunic and cloak that are not torn?"

Dumbfounded, I could neither move nor respond.

"Come," she said gently but firmly, taking me by the hand.

Speechless, I followed her obediently, still not comprehending what was happening. I stood by in helpless wonder as Bernice slipped into clean, whole garments. I would have slumped to the ground from shock had not her strong, young arms caught me—arms which just a few, short hours ago had been limp and lifeless as her mother had thrust her weak body into my outstretched hands. Now she was the one in command as she supported and steadied me, then eased me gently to the mat on the floor of her bedroom.

I sat there weakly, still in shock, as I surveyed her smooth, silky skin—not a blemish on it. Not even a telltale scar on her face from the ugly lacerations that had been so inflamed that morning.

"What happened?" I whispered.

"I don't know," she replied with shining eyes. "I never felt like this before. I feel new all over. I'm a different person."

Moments before, Simone was on her way home from gathering mint and mustard on the hillside when she heard the now familiar voices of the students of her husband's guest, the Healer. The men were gesturing toward a woman lying prostrate on the ground at the feet of the Healer. Her form looked strangely familiar to Simone. Why, it looked like, yes, it was Justa! She must have been annoying the men, for they were loudly urging their Teacher to send her away.

Wailing and weeping shamelessly, Justa cried out repeatedly, "Lord, Son of David!"

How strange and out of place those words had sounded coming from Justa's Gentile lips. The Stranger ignored her plea as He turned, seemingly indifferent to her appeal.

Again Justa cried out through her tears, "Have mercy on me and heal my daughter, my only child!"

The Healer looked down before Him upon the bowed form of the desperate woman and said, "I cannot give the children's meat to the dogs—no, not even to the puppies and the family pets." Even Simone could hear the pathos in the Man's voice that took the sting from the apparent insult.

Hope, born of courage and faith, sprang up within Justa's heart. Had He not said "puppies" rather than "wild dogs," the usual term with which the Jews referred to the despised Gentiles?

Startled but undaunted, Justa answered, "A little crumb for my daughter will not deprive the children."

At the display of such boldness, the Healer reached out and laid His hand upon Justa's shoulder, gently raising her to her feet. With kingly grace and a heavenly radiance surrounding Him, He looked directly into Justa's eyes.

"The demon is gone from your daughter. Go home. She is well."

Justa had asked for only a little crumb, and that was what the Master had given her. But only crumbs had met her every need and made her daughter whole.

Lois I. Sink

The Sound of a Trumpet

Stuart Chambers paused beneath the awning and lit a cigarette. The pavement, wet with recent rain, reflected the glare of streetlights. Cars and buses made rapid slashing sounds in accompaniment to the clicking footfalls of passersby.

Though it was past seven, Stuart knew the crowds would not diminish. Indeed, by ten when he was due back at the club, the streets would be teeming with life. People eager for a good time would happily make their way to the city's nightspots. Many would come to the Lavender Lounge where he worked.

The rehearsal had gone well, and now was time for supper and some relaxation before the long night of work. He picked up his trumpet and fell into step with the crowd. Funny, how playing his beloved trumpet had become work. What had once been a joy now meant long tedious hours, noisy, smoke–filled clubs, flowing liquor. He had never become used to the smell of alcohol. A familiar loneliness surrounded him more closely than the elbowing crowd.

Somehow he had hoped coming back here to the city of his beginnings would help. When he had first begun touring with the group, he had known the exhilaration of success and excitement of new places. It had meant enough money to buy what he wanted.

Then came Elena, with her sparkling winsomeness, her beautiful sea–green eyes and warm spirit. And their marriage had been a good one—at least for a while. But gradually Elena became annoyed with his continual absence from home. They argued some. Then more and more they began taking separate courses in life, growing further and further apart. Stuart watched it happening and hated it, but he was powerless to do anything to change it.

How long would it be before Elena walked out on him for good? How long before his world fell completely apart? Stuart sighed as he took a place at the counter of a small restaurant.

The waitress brought tea and a nondescript sandwich that he nibbled without tasting. Morosely he watched the rain drip along the wide window before him. Meaningless, incessant drops washed silently over the glass—like the days of his life, he thought. The rain seemed to give him kinship, comfort, and when it ended he felt as though a good friend had left him.

He paid for the tea and, gripping the handle of his instrument case, headed for the hotel. Perhaps what he needed was a good rest. Turning down Dunham Street he took in the lighted shops and cafes, but there was no easing of the burden inside. He walked slowly, dreading the impending silence of his own room. Life had become a monotonous routine. And without Elena? He shook his head, not wanting to complete the thought.

Suddenly he hesitated. He could hear music, faint at first but growing louder. Even before he identified it, the glimmer of recognition rose in his mind. He paused by a crowded condiment shop and waited.

The steady beat of a drum struck a familiar chord. Fascinated, he watched them, coming closer and closer, marching down the wide street. The flags came first. Flaring boldly in the night wind came the colors he had seen so often in his youth—blue–bordered red with a blazing yellow star. Men and women in dark blue uniforms marched steadily, heads held high, a rhythmic buoyancy in their step.

The bandsmen played a song he knew well. It was a strong, good sound. But there was a dreamlike quality to this whole thing. A Salvation Army band marching to the street service? All that was so long ago!

Stuart found himself following slowly, as though he were sleepwalking. Many people had gathered by the time he arrived. He was glad because he could watch and listen unnoticed in the crowd.

Someone was praying. The men held their caps in their hands and a hush fell over the group. Then the singing began. Stuart listened to the blending voices lift a lively refrain, the band playing softly in accompaniment. *"Jesus the name high over all . . ."* Yes, he remembered. Inaudibly he mouthed the words, a panorama of experiences returning to his mind. How long had it been? Ten years? Fifteen?

Suddenly Stuart caught sight of a young lad, perhaps seventeen, with blond hair and gray eyes. A cornet was set to his full mouth, and his fingers rose and fell over the valves of his instrument. He seemed to possess an air of assurance and dignity in his uniform with its braid at each shoulder.

From the streetlight Stuart could see the boy's eyes glow with a warmth and brightness that made his own heart jump. Could it be? Yes . . . he could see himself again, the Stuart Chambers of long ago. He tried to look away, but like a magnet his eyes returned to the youth. The cornet was lowered now, for the captain was preaching. The pages of the hand–held Bible fluttered in the wind as the officer's voice penetrated the din of people passing.

"'There is a way that seems right to a man, but the end of it is death,'" The captain's luminous eyes seemed to pierce Stuart's own. "Jesus said, 'I am the Way, the Truth and the Life . . .'"

Stuart felt the words sear deep into his soul. Once he had known the Way, the Truth. How long ago! But like an arrow God's words went straight to his heart. Once he had stood, perhaps on that very corner, with trumpet in hand, playing the same tunes, witnessing to the experience of knowing Jesus Christ.

Yet, more than ten years later, he was walking busy streets with emptiness and longing in his soul. How he had drifted so far from home Stuart couldn't tell for sure. His brow furrowed as he cast back in memory.

Perhaps it had been the thing he loved the most. He remembered how his ambitions as a musician had crowded out everything else. He no longer had time for worship or Bible reading. Eventually even the band at the corps could no longer hold him. He was reaching out for greater things.

Stuart shook his head as the band got ready again to play. How could he have allowed it to happen? Life was in that ring of men and women who loved and served God. And he, Stuart, had stepped outside of it. He was an onlooker—a poor lad peering hungrily into a candy store, knowing he had no money to purchase even the smallest bit of sweet.

The music began, softly at first, and the strain caught in Stuart's mind. A hundred times he had played the hymn—*On a hill far away stood an old rugged cross* . . . The crowd milling in front of him grew quiet as the music lingered over them.

Without really being aware that he had opened his case, Stuart's own trumpet was in his hand. Very softly he began to play with the band . . . *the emblem of suffering and shame. But I love that old cross where the dearest and best for a world of lost sinners was slain* . . .

"For you, Stuart," came the Savior's words in his heart—"for you." Stuart's eyes grew cloudy as the music welled up from his heart and flowed through the trumpet.

Suddenly he became aware that there was no other sound but his own. The bandsmen and the audience stood hushed, their eyes intent on him. *I will cling to the old rugged cross, and exchange it some day for a crown.* He let the trumpet fall from his lips and dropped his head as the tears stung his eyes.

"Oh, my God!" he cried without words.

Stuart felt a warm hand on his shoulder. He knew before he lifted his head that the young bandsman, so like himself, was standing there. His gray eyes were as warm as his handclasp.

Stuart smiled through his tears. "I guess it's time I came home," he said, looking into the boy's glowing face.

"He waits for you, sir," said the boy quietly.

Long after the sound of the trumpet on the street had stilled, the music of God's loving grace filled Stuart's soul. Whatever lay ahead now was in God's hands—God, the Master Conductor!

Lt. Colonel Marlene Chase

Autumn

Even when the trees have just surrendered

to the harvest time,

Forfeiting their leaves in late September

and sending us inside;

Still, I notice You when change begins

and I am braced for colder winds;

I will offer thanks for what has been

and what's to come.

The Tenth

He wasn't much to look at, but he had a spirit as fresh as spring water, and just as sparkling. Grandpa called him "Fledge" and said it was all right if I wanted to call him "Uncle Fledge."

Uncle Fledge was as much a part of me as the toad in my pocket, the pebbles I skimmed across the slippery pond and the sorghum cane I peeled with my front teeth. He and his son Tobe lived on my grandparents' place, where I spent my summer vacations. Tobe and I were the same age, and he was my constant companion.

Uncle Fledge day–labored for a living. But Grandpa let him have a couple of acres so he and Tobe could have a garden and a corn patch of their own. In return, Uncle Fledge always gave a tenth of every-thing he had to the Lord. Poor as he was, he found someone poorer than he to give the tenth to. That wasn't hard to do among his day–laboring neighbors with their large families.

The gale blew in one night in September, just before school was to start. It was the year Tobe and I were twelve. For weeks we had enjoyed Indian summer, the days running one after the other like rip-ples along a sunny shore. Every morning Uncle Fledge went to his corn patch and walked the rows. "A few more days and it'll be ready to pull, boys," he told Tobe and me. There was pleasure and excitement on his face. "Best crop we ever had." He slapped Tobe on the shoul-der. "That means new clothes for you and a good winter for us both."

That morning when I awoke, the wind was whipping from the east, wet and strong. "It's a gale, boys." Uncle Fledge was almost fran-tic. "We gotta get the corn in before it wastes." In no time we had the corn gathering underway. Uncle Fledge shuffled up one row and down another, stripping the rustling stalks, while Tobe and I piled the corn in baskets.

Uncle Fledge was scurrying faster than I ever saw a human move, pulling and slinging that corn. "That gale's strengthening. It's gonna blow us right outta this patch before we know what it's about."

He was right. No sooner had the corn gathering begun than we were driven to cover. We barely got the few loaded baskets in the barn before the storm broke.

Standing by the stove in the kitchen, Uncle Fledge said, "Well, at least we saved the Lord's tenth, I guess."

"Pa!" Tobe's eyes blazed. "You ain't gonna give away the last ear of corn we have, are you?"

Uncle Fledge just looked at Tobe, then started to shape some corn pones with one hand while patting them firm with the other. As he dropped them in the hot grease, he spoke. "In all your twelve years, boy, have you ever gone hungry?"

"No, Pa." Tobe's voice sounded like the sizzling grease. "But we sure as shooting will this winter if you give all our corn away." He whirled and left the room. Uncle Fledge shook his white head.

"That boy don't have a speck of faith." His voice sounded like the wind moaning around the house.

I went off to find Tobe. He was in the shed sprawled across a cot. His arm was flung across his eyes, and I guessed he had been crying. I sat down in the chair and waited. Tobe would talk when he was ready.

Finally he sat up and looked at me. His eyes were red. "Pa gives our stuff away to the first beggar who comes along!" His voice was shot through with anger.

"Yeah, I know, Tobe." That was all I could think to say. I felt sorry for him. I knew why he didn't want Uncle Fledge to give all their corn away. They wouldn't have any cornmeal for bread that winter.

The rain was still galloping in when Uncle Fledge's voice rang from the kitchen. "Boys, dinner's ready."

The springs creaked as Tobe jumped from the cot. "Better eat while there's something to eat." He trotted to the kitchen with me at his heels.

We all sat quietly as we feasted on golden crunchy corn pones. Tobe didn't say any more about the corn, but I knew he would keep worrying. He was too quiet when we played dominoes after dinner. I felt so sorry for Tobe that I didn't even try to beat him this time.

The summer break soon ended, and I wouldn't see Tobe or Uncle Fledge again until Thanksgiving time. But I would think of them often. Would they starve? No, I knew Grandpa wouldn't allow that. But I also knew they would have a hard time.

Sometimes I did without lunch at school and sneaked the money away in a little jar hidden in my clothes closet. I meant to carry it to Tobe so he could buy some cornmeal. By the time Thanksgiving came, I had saved six dollars, and I was thrilled to be heading back to the farm to spend the holiday with my grandparents.

"How are Tobe and Uncle Fledge getting along?" I asked when Grandpa and Grandma met me at the train depot.

Grandpa laughed. "Just fine. Mr. Hudson strained his back a month ago. So he hired Fledge to do the lifting and the heavy chores at the store. He declares he won't ever be able to lift or carry any-more, so it looks like Fledge has a permanent job."

Later, as I headed over to see Tobe, I met him coming down the trail toward me.

"Knew you'd be coming," he grinned. "Did you know Pa's working for Mr. Hudson now? And I'm building 'coon traps. Gonna sell the hides." After looking at me a minute, he turned a cartwheel. Then he straightened up and looked at me again. "Guess we won't go hungry this winter, after all."

I felt the crisp dollar bills in my pocket. I smiled back, but I didn't say a word. I'd buy Tobe something nice for Christmas.

"Come on. You can help me finish the traps." Tobe led the way back into the woods.

We worked awhile, then I leaned back and said, "Tobe, let's talk."

"Okay," he agreed. "What'll we talk about?"

"Uncle Fledge and the Lord's corn. Do you 'reckon it was the Lord that got Uncle Fledge that job?"

"Shucks, no!" Tobe shook his head. "Course, that's what Pa believes. But you don't think the Lord would sprain Mr. Hudson's back, do you?"

He had me there. I couldn't see the Lord doing that.

Tobe and I were sitting on the front porch that evening when Uncle Fledge came driving up in a pickup.

"What's Pa doing bringing Mr. Hudson's truck home?" Tobe's eyes were puzzled, but he didn't have to wonder long.

Uncle Fledge called. "Hey, you boys come and help me unload this cornmeal."

Tobe stared at me as we ran. "Did you hear that? He said 'cornmeal!'" There were six sacks of it.

"Where'd you get all that cornmeal, Pa?"

"Mr. Hudson gave it to me." Uncle Fledge's smile lit up his face. "The sacks got torn and he said they wouldn't sell. I'll sew the sacks up when we get them in the house."

Tobe was stopped in his tracks. He just stood there looking kind of dazed. "Six sacks of cornmeal!"

"Remember the Lord's tenth of corn, Tobe?" asked Uncle Fledge, looking mighty satisfied.

"You bet I do," laughed Tobe. "And this is already ground!"

Josie Patrick

In Due Season

Sarah threw down her hoe and stamped her foot angrily on the ground. "I'm not going to break my back digging in this old garden. It will take forever to get rid of all these weeds and clods."

Her brother Joe stopped to wipe his face with a faded sleeve. "I don't see how you can talk about quitting, Sarah. Not when you've been named after Grandma."

Sarah knew what her brother meant. Their grandmother worked tirelessly, year after year, to make her dream come true. An ordinary person would have become discouraged long ago, but Sarah Josepha Hale was not an ordinary person.

Young Sarah pulled her braids away from her neck and glared at Joe with a defiant look on her flushed face. "I think Grandma is foolish to keep sending those letters. How many years has she been writing them?"

"Ever since I can remember and long before I was born," Joe replied, then added, "You had better not tell her you gave up on your garden after just a few hours. You said you were going to raise enough vegetables for us and for all the hungry children around here whose fathers have gone off to war, remember?"

"But I didn't know it would take so long," grumbled Sarah, picking up the hoe once more. "And I'm getting a blister!"

The sky was scarlet with sunset when Sarah wearily trudged home. Only one handful of pumpkin seeds had been planted. More hard work awaited her tomorrow, and the next day, and the day after that. "I've done enough!" she murmured rebelliously.

Sarah knew where she would find her grandmother—at her desk, dipping pen in ink to write *Philadelphia, Pennsylvania, July 15, 1863* at the top of each page before she began to shape her neat, pleading words and sentences.

Mrs. Hale looked up as her granddaughter entered. "Come here and let me give you a hug, Sarah. What a glorious day you must have had, working outside surrounded by all the beauty God has created for us!"

"I didn't see any beauty," Sarah answered sulkily. "All I saw was dirt. I'm tired, Grandma. I want to quit."

"All of us feel like giving up sometimes, Sarah, but if we believe we are working at something worthwhile, we must persevere."

"But suppose all my hard work in the hot sun is for nothing. Suppose there is not enough rain or too much rain or a blight or—"

Her grandmother laughed. "Be optimistic, Sarah. Be hopeful. There is a Scripture passage that encourages me whenever I feel like quitting. I'm sure you know it. Let's say it together. *And let us not be weary in well doing . . .*"

Sarah joined in reluctantly, *"for in due season we shall reap, if we faint not"* (Gal. 6:9, KJV).

Mrs. Hale touched the stack of freshly written letters on her desk. "That message has kept me at my task for forty years, Sarah. It inspires me to take up this pen every day and keep writing to our congressmen and governors and presidents."

Forty years! Sarah pictured the giant stack of mail that had passed from her grandmother's desk to Washington, D.C.

"Don't you get tired, Grandma?"

"Of course, I do," she replied. "After editing a big publication like *Godey's Lady's Book* all day, I would like to come home and relax. But this is something that needs to be done. And I'm going to keep on telling our lawmakers that it must be done." She smiled at the discouraged girl. "Look out the window, Sarah. What do you see?"

Sarah peered into the twilight. "Grass and trees. Sky. A cornfield. An apple orchard. Cows coming back to the barn to be milked."

"And all over this nation, in our twenty–nine states and in our territories, people can look out on beautiful, bountiful scenes like that. We are so blessed, Sarah! Don't you see why I feel the way I do—that the United States should have a national day of thanksgiving every year?"

Sarah hesitated. There was a question she wanted to ask, but she feared her grandmother would think it was sacrilegious. At last she blurted it out.

"Grandma, if God wanted you to keep working at this, wouldn't He have let you succeed long ago? Wouldn't He have helped you?"

"But He has!" Mrs. Hale's voice was joyful. "He has opened the way for me to have the time I desperately needed. You see, Sarah, I have always felt strongly about this, but when my husband died I had small children to support, and that demanded my attention."

Sarah had heard of those years. "You had to take in sewing."

"Yes. And how I hated it! I have always disliked sewing. And, worst of all, I had to work far into the night. I felt frustrated. I wanted to help establish a national day of thanksgiving, but I had to sew every minute."

Sarah began to understand. "So when you were asked to be the editor of a magazine, you thought it was God's way of giving you some free time."

"Exactly. It meant my evenings were my own. I could begin to write my letters. And, in addition, I could write editorials."

"But, Grandma, why don't you stop now? Most of the states have started observing a day of thanksgiving."

"Yes, you're right. I think some of those legislators finally got tired of reading my letters. But I want a national holiday, Sarah, like the one our nation had when our first president, George Washington, proclaimed the last Thursday in November 1789 as a day to give thanks. That's why I've written to so many presidents—Polk, Taylor, Filmore, Pierce, Buchanan—"

"And they didn't listen."

"No, they didn't. But now Mr. Lincoln is president. I've sent letters to him. He has so much on his mind, but maybe . . ."

Sarah looked at the ink stains on her grandmother's fingers and then at the dirt stains on her own. "Planting a vegetable garden just doesn't seem very worthwhile compared to what you're doing, Grandma."

"But helping things grow is a way of helping God with His wonderful plan. And when you see those seeds become plants, and when you watch those lovely vegetables ripen, then you'll be so thankful to the Creator. Now just think how wonderful it would be if this year the twenty–three million people in our land could have services of joy and thanksgiving on one special day."

"Grandmother!" Joe burst into the room, waving a newspaper. "You've done it! President Lincoln listened. Look, here is his proclamation: *"Now, therefore, be it known that I do set apart Thursday, the sixth day of August next, to be observed as a day for national thanksgiving."*"

Sarah clapped her hands. "Oh, Grandmother, how wonderful! You did it! Now you can rest."

"Not yet." Sarah's grandmother wiped her pen and placed the stopper on her inkwell, then rose to her feet. "I must visit Mr. Lincoln in person. Our national Thanksgiving should be observed on the day that President Washington selected—the last Thursday in November. I won't stop until it's done. And, Sarah," she turned a steady gaze on her granddaughter, "you must never think of giving up just because a job is hard."

"I won't," Sarah promised. "I certainly won't give up on my garden, Grandma. After all, we just have to have pumpkins ready for pies on the last Thursday in November."

Margaret Chaplin Campbell

The Church Bell
of the Two Sabbaths

Many years ago, the tiny and isolated village of Krakus boasted two unusual attractions—one, a beautiful church; the other, a small but full-voiced bell, which called the faithful to daily prayers and Sabbath worship. Eli, the bell-ringer, was unusual himself. He was the only Jewish man in Krakus, and he eked out a living, along with his wife Rebecca and their eight children, on a modest piece of ground just outside the village.

Father Josephus, the lively old priest at the church, regarded Eli as a brother—and not only because God was the father of them both. The two men discussed every topic that interested them, sometimes agreeing, oftentimes not, but always with respect and love.

One morning, before the sun had even thought of rising, a frantic message came to Eli: Bring a wagonload of hay to the church immediately. Rebecca roused the sleeping children, and they heaped the wagon with hay while Eli hitched up the horse. Then the whole family climbed aboard and helped urge the still drowsy horse through the quiet streets.

An impatient Father Josephus met them outside. His hands shook as he handed Eli a large gold goblet with a lid. "The Blessed Sacrament is in here," he explained quickly. "Will you hide it in the woods by your house?"

Eli agreed and pushed it beneath the hay. Then the priest buried a wooden box filled with church documents under the hay, too. He explained that a murderous band of Cossacks were in the nearest city looting and burning churches. He had to protect the church's most precious belongings.

Rebecca begged the priest to come home with them, but he refused, saying that he could not abandon his church and warning them to be careful. If the Cossacks suspected they had the gold goblet, their lives would be forfeited.

Suddenly Eli jumped down. "We must save the bell, too." Father Josephus shook his head. A bell would be too hard to hide. But Eli persisted. Who would think of looking for a church bell in a Jew's house?

Eli, Rebecca and Father Josephus lowered the bell gently from the belfry and placed it on the wagon. They heaped hay over it, then set the children around the bell and covered them, too. Eli clucked to the horse, who moved even slower with his extra burden. He promised to return as soon as possible to help Father Josephus defend the other church treasures.

But as they creaked down the dusty road, a stranger on a snorting horse reined up beside the wagon. "What do you have there, peasant?"

Eli's mouth grew dry. "Just . . . hay."

The horseman drew his sword. "I'll soon discover what treasure you're hiding."

"How did you guess our treasure so quickly?" Rebecca said with a careless laugh. "You must be very clever." Quickly, before the greedy rider could plunge his saber into the hay, she roused one child after another. They sat up, innocently rubbing their eyes.

"This old fool has as many mouths to feed as the Tsar," the horseman called to a band of uniformed, rough-looking fellows who had cantered up beside him. "We'll find better treasure in Krakus than your sallow-faced brats!" he roared, galloping away.

Eli dared a relieved smile at his wife as he pointed his plodding horse toward the woods. There they hid the gold chalice and the wooden box among the green bushes. When they returned home, Eli unhitched the horse and rode slowly back toward town, promising the poor beast a long rest soon. He'd leave the bell on the wagon and return it as soon as the Cossacks left.

But by the time Eli reached the church, it was afire. The vestments, the crucifixes, the candlesticks were gone, and his beloved Father Josephus lay in front of the altar, a dagger through his heart. Sorrowfully Eli returned home, and his family mourned their friend according to their own ways—seven days of sitting *shiva* on low pillows while wearing no shoes. Then they retrieved the church property from the woods and hid it in their house.

One long, lonely year followed another. Eli never got used to the loss of Father Josephus or to passing his days without ringing the bell. Finally he and his sons hung it on a crosspiece next to his house. He rang it once a day to call his children in from the fields, but from sundown Friday to sundown Saturday the bell remained silent. On the Jewish Sabbath, no one—not even a bell—worked.

Many years later, when Eli had grown quite gray, a priest arrived at his house and announced that he wanted to rebuild the church. Father Josephus had been his uncle. Eli and Rebecca pulled out the gold goblet and wooden box from their dusty hiding places. Then Eli took him outside to see the bell and promised to return it as soon as the belfry was ready.

All the villagers helped rebuild the church. They, too, missed Father Josephus and wanted to show their love for him. When the church was finished, it was not so showy, but the priest did not care.

"Your good hearts and unselfish works are the offerings that God really wants," he told the people.

Eli, Rebecca and their children (some now with children of their own) hauled the bell back to the church where many eager hands helped hang it. The new priest insisted that Eli ring the bell just as he had done many years before. Eli agreed and pulled long and hard at the bell rope. The deep, melodious summons was as loud and clear as always, and the villagers clapped their hands at its familiar voice.

Eli's smile was bright when he finished, but he rubbed his shoulder and grimaced in pain. He, and everyone else, realized then that he was too old to be the bell–ringer anymore.

A deep silence fell over the crowd. Who would be their next bell–ringer?

Just then Aaron, Eli's grandson, stepped forward. "I would like to be your bell–ringer." A cry of agreement erupted, but then Aaron added, "Although I would not ring the bell on Saturday, just like my grandfather."

When another youngster offered to ring the bell on Saturday, the priest shook his head. "I think the church bell should rest then, too. Its silence will remind us each week just how much Eli and his family have helped us all."

Eli smiled to himself and whispered to the priest, "Father, now the church bell will observe *two* Sabbaths, and God's holy day of rest will be twice blessed in our village."

Sharlya Gold

When Is a Revival Not a Revival?

Pastor Jefferson threw his briefcase on the parsonage table with a bang. "Well," he said disgustedly, "if that was a revival tonight, it sure didn't seem like it. Not a single seeker. Not one person seemed to make a move toward God."

Molly wiped the frown from her face and put on the smile she kept for occasions such as this. She turned to her husband and put her arms around his neck to kiss the discouragement from his lips.

"Really, honey, it's not that bad. I've often heard you say that you cannot judge the results of a revival meeting by the size of its congregation or by the number who come forward. Where is our evangelist?"

"Harry is talking to some drunk who staggered in during the meeting. I told him to lock up when he got rid of the man." He sighed. "Think of the money we spent on advertising, and we haven't a thing to show for it."

Back at the church Harry Alexander sat in a pew, face–to–face with the man who was under the influence of alcohol.

"I tell you, *Reverner,* I'm not a drunk!" the man kept insisting. "I'm a broken man who has lost everything!"

Harry wondered just how drunk the man was, so he asked, "Tell me, what brought you to the meeting tonight?"

The man reached into his overcoat pocket and after several fumbling attempts managed to bring out a small bottle of pills. "Reverner, I was alone under a streetlight, and I said to myself, 'Why don't I just take all these sleeping pills and never wake up?'"

He handed the bottle to Harry.

"What stopped you?" Harry asked the man, who was sobering up a little.

"There was this kid selling papers, and he comes up to me and says that there's a big meeting down at his church on the corner, and shows me a story about it in the paper. So I bought a paper and read where you said the Bible has a solution to every man's problem. I came to find out if it has one for mine."

"There's no doubt about it," Harry said. "This Book has a solution to every man's problems, including yours. Now, tell me, what is your problem?"

The man began, "I have a good job. I live in a nice house. I have a good, intelligent wife, two girls, and a baby son. But my wife is going to divorce me, and when her lawyers get through with me, I won't have anything left."

"Why is she divorcing you?"

"We just can't get along. We fight like cats and dogs."

Harry encouraged the man to continue his account, and for many minutes the man bared his soul.

"That's it, Reverend," he said at last. "I've leveled with you. Now, is there anything in that Book that can help me?"

"Yes, there certainly is. I think your verse is in the New Testament, Matthew 5:39: *But I tell you, do not resist an evil person. If someone strikes you on the right cheek, turn to him the other also.* Those are the words of Jesus, the Mender of broken lives."

"Come on, now, Reverend. There's nothing in that verse that could help anyone, let alone someone in my shoes."

With open Bible between them, Harry Alexander spent another hour counseling the man, who appeared earnest and in need of help.

Finally, the man got to his feet. "Reverend, let me take your hand. My name is Jack McMahon. I was brought up right, but I went wrong somewhere. I promise you I will do my best to take your advice and stand on that verse, with God as my witness."

Jack McMahon stepped out into what had looked like the darkest night of his life, but now he had one ray of hope—in his hand was a New Testament with one verse underlined.

Jack was hoping everyone would be in bed when he got home, but every light in the house was on. He opened the door softly. His baby son was crying in the crib. Jack picked up the child with unpracticed hands, patting his back gently. He took the bottle of juice that his wife had prepared and sat down in the rocker with the baby.

Soon the boy's cries hushed as he fell asleep. His two sisters tip–toed out of their room to see what had brought such a calm to the house. Jack put the baby in his crib, then did something he hadn't done for a long while. He motioned for the girls to come and sit on his lap, and his soft voice soon had them sound asleep also. He put each one to bed with a kiss.

Jack climbed into his own bed and gently put his arm around Mary, only to be rewarded with a sharp jab from her elbow. He held back the angry words, remembering his verse: *If someone strikes you on the right cheek, turn to him the other also.*

The next morning, Mary made breakfast—the coffee was weak, the toast was burned and the eggs ran. But she didn't care; she was getting a divorce anyway. Jack remembered his verse and whispered to her, "Honey, that's just the way I like it."

At the office, Jack remembered one of the things Reverend Alexander had said: "Flowers were made for the living." So that evening he brought home a dozen red roses for his wife. Again, he paid attention to the baby and even got down on the carpet to play a game with the girls.

Mary phoned her mother the next morning. "Mom, Jack sure is putting on an act. He's feeding the baby and playing with the girls. They had the time of their lives, riding him around like a horse. He hasn't smoked one of his stinking cigars for two days now. Last night he brought home a bouquet of roses—first time that I can remember. Instead of reading the paper or staring at the television, he's been acting like a father. Too bad it's about to end. The last two mornings the coffee was weak and the toast was burned, and all he said was 'Thanks for the breakfast, that's just the way I like it.' What an actor!"

"Mary, listen to me." Her mother paused to give weight to her words. "Maybe it's not just an act. Jack may be really trying to save your home. Remember, there are a lot of people who have been praying for you and Jack. Please don't be in such a hurry to get your divorce that you don't give him a chance if he's really trying to change."

Jack continued to follow the evangelist's advice. At the office, he put Mary's picture back on his desk and began to enumerate all her good points. He went to an exclusive dress shop, chose a beautiful blue gown and had it gift–wrapped. When he came home, he presented the gift to Mary, saying, "Here is something for your birthday. It's late, I know, but better late than never."

Mary threw the box in the corner. Just part of his act, she told herself. That evening, however, while Jack was washing the dishes and putting the children to bed, her curiosity got the best of her and she opened the discarded gift. When she saw the expensive gown, she realized that if Jack was putting on an act, it was costing him money.

What if he was not playing a game? What if he was really trying? Even if she got all the alimony her lawyers had told her to ask for, would the children be as happy and well–adjusted without their father? Maybe her mother was right. She knew the church had been praying for them.

Mary made up her mind. She was going to find out if Jack was just playing a game. If he was, she would call his bluff.

She put on the blue gown, checked her appearance in the mirror and walked into the room where Jack was reading. The look in his eyes convinced her he was not acting, so she sat on his lap and put her arms around him the way she did when they were first married.

Jack held her tight. His body shook with sobs. She locked her arms tighter around him and began to weep herself.

"Jack," she whispered softly, "can you forgive me for being the worst wife any man ever had?"

"You don't have it right, Mary," he answered, still sobbing. "Can you forgive me for being the worst husband any woman ever had?"

They stayed entwined in each other's arms as only true lovers can after a long absence. Finally Jack spoke. "Mary, now that we have asked each other's forgiveness and reaffirmed our vows, let's get down on our knees and ask God's forgiveness and promise Him we will serve Him."

Together they knelt and prayed. That was when they heard the patter of little feet, and two little girls cuddled beside them. "Will you pray with us, too, Daddy?" they asked.

It was a year later that Harry Alexander was called back by the pastor to the same church on the corner to conduct another revival. Harry was puzzled, however, by the pastor's enthusiastic and somewhat mysterious invitation to return. "You won't believe your eyes!" was all Pastor Jefferson would say, but Harry remembered how very disappointed the pastor had been after the first meeting a year ago.

As Harry drove up to the church with Pastor Jefferson, he found the parking lot full. The old building had been repaired and painted, the grass was trimmed, and new shrubs had been planted. People were filing into the church. "Sure have been some changes around here since I last saw it," he remarked.

The pastor nodded, smiled at Harry and asked, "Would you like to know what brought all these about?"

When Harry opened the church door, a happy, energetic couple walked up to greet him. "I'll bet you don't recognize me, Reverend," the man said as he pumped his hand. "I'm the Sunday school superintendent here now. This is my wife, Mary. She teaches the young marrieds' Bible class. We owe you an awful lot!"

As the evangelist held the hands of the man and woman, tears of joy began to stream down his face. He exclaimed, "Praise God, it's Jack McMahon! It looks like last year was a real revival after all!"

Art Fee

Open the Door and See All the People

"In all honesty, Don, would it be better if I got sick and couldn't go? You know I can run a fever when I need to, so you wouldn't have to lie. If you're at all concerned that I might not make a good impression, just say the word and I'll throw up."

"Ellen, you'll be fine. Don't worry." He gave her a smile that was part tenderness and part amusement.

He's afraid I'm going to mess up this deal for him, Ellen thought. *Why did he marry me in the first place?* It was her turn at the sink as she shot the question at the girl in the mirror. Don had known he was going to be a minister when he proposed. If she was so wildly unsuited to be a preacher's wife, why didn't he realize it before he talked her into supporting him through three years of seminary?

A week ago, when Don had been asked to preach at Bethany Church, the chairman had said, "We would like to talk to you and your wife about perhaps becoming our pastor." She had resented the "and your wife" when Don reported the conversation. Why should they pass judgment on her? She wasn't applying for a job in their church.

"Ellen, they just want to get acquainted. Can't you see that it would be difficult for a church to accept a man's ministry if they didn't like his wife?"

Ellen was a novice church member, unlike Don, who grew up in a parsonage. Her family did not attend church, and until she had become a Christian while in college, her experience with church had been of the Christmas and Easter variety. Now Don talked of sharing her life with strangers.

"Show me where it says in the marriage ceremony that I'm taking on some kind of position called 'preacher's wife.' You should have made that a little clearer, Don. I seem to remember a lot of talk about love and how cute I am and how you can't live without me, but how does that stuff fit on a resumé when I apply to be a preacher's wife?"

"That's just it, honey. You tricked me, and I'm sure you can hood-wink the—ooof—" His sentence had been stopped short by a whallop in the stomach.

Don was already warming up the car when Ellen climbed in beside him. Her mind raced. As always, when she was faced with a threatening situation, she put her imagination to work. What was the absolute worst thing that could happen? She would picture it, in living color, gritting her teeth, and find out if she could survive. She figured if the worst didn't kill her, anything less was manageable.

During the inquisition that was to follow, what would be the worst thing she could possibly do that would cover herself with embarrass-ment and her husband with shame? She didn't know much about the Bible, but if they should quiz her, she'd be honest. People don't hate you for being dumb.

Would it matter that she couldn't sing? She loved music and danced pretty well. Oh, right, that fits into the picture of your ideal preacher's wife. Besides, she wasn't about to start snapping her fingers and bebopping to hymns.

What she might do, most likely, would be to disgrace herself at dinner. Nervous, talking too much, she might just spill something on her dress and say something she shouldn't. She imagined how quiet everyone would get. Don's ears would turn red, and he would help her mop up. At that moment would they decide that her husband couldn't be their minister—because of her?

Don wanted to be the minister of this church, and she doubted if she could stand it if she were the cause of his not receiving a call.

Their car pulled into the church parking lot, and Don jumped out almost before it came to a stop.

"Listen, Ellen, I have to rush right in and find out the order of service. You'll be okay, huh? You look beautiful, honey. Everyone will love you."

If he was so sure, why was only the bottom part of his face smiling? There was a deep crease between his eyes, and his large hands were clumsy as he snatched up his Bible and notebook. She'd seen him through enough finals in the seminary to recognize when he was about to face one of the biggest tests of his life. This time, though, he had her marks to worry about as well as his own.

What if she crawled in the backseat and covered up with the football blanket? It might be awkward for Don not to know where his wife was when the board wanted to meet her—but maybe less painful than presenting her. At least she knew she wouldn't talk too much—her throat ached with tightness and her voice would probably come out as a squeak.

As Ellen pushed through the heavy door, a tall woman came toward her. She was elderly, but not the grandmother type. She was more the I–hope–I–look–like–that–when–I'm–her–age type.

"You're Ellen," she said. "I'm Betty Johnson. My husband was the pastor here for twenty–two years before he died last May." She put out her hand and Ellen took it. "My dear girl, your hands are freezing." She looked closely at Ellen. "You're scared, aren't you? Come with me a few minutes." She excused them both with some gracious words to the others who had been waiting to greet Ellen, and they went into one of the Sunday school rooms.

Mrs. Johnson motioned Ellen to a folding chair and sat in front of her, so close their knees almost touched. "Will it be all right if I pray for you, Ellen?"

Ellen nodded and hoped she wouldn't be expected to join in. She certainly knew how to pray, but only privately, never where this charming, poised person would hear.

When Mrs. Johnson spoke, Ellen raised her head quickly, thinking another person had entered the room.

81

"Father, this little girl is scared green," Mrs. Johnson began. "Remember how I was, Lord?" She chuckled. "Oh my, I don't believe You ever thought I'd make it, did You? Well, now what I'd like to ask is, if You'd help Ellen learn quickly—right now, as a matter of fact— what You let me muddle through for years before I found out. Lord, please show her that all the folks in this church have more important things on their minds than watching her. Amen."

Mrs. Johnson finished and was getting up, but Ellen's head stayed bowed as she struggled with what she had heard. Was she really making the proverbial mountain out of a molehill?

They left the room and went back to the foyer of the church. Several people were entering and Betty Johnson introduced each one to Ellen. She didn't just give their names but a sentence or two of introduction. "Mrs. Moore is the world's best seamstress—hard to believe she didn't start sewing until her husband died two years ago," and "Mr. Harvey, meet Ellen Matthews—her husband will be preaching this morning. Mr. Harvey sits up front and takes notes so he can preach the message to his wife when he gets home."

And so it went, until the organ summoned them to the sanctuary. When Betty offered to share her songbook, Ellen sang vigorously, with no lump in her throat. She didn't know if God had answered Betty's prayer—right now, in fact—or if she had become so interested in the people she met that she forgot to worry about what they might think of her.

Perhaps when she and Don stood at the door at the end of the service, there would be someone with cold hands for her to love and help.

Edna Thorpe

Jane Doe

Her green plastic hospital wristband seemed to shout it: "Jane Doe!" She had been admitted to the hospital at midnight with a concussion. They called her Jane Doe because she had no identification or personal information.

The nurses had put her to bed with the hope that all would be well in the morning. When morning came, it brought only the police with a bundle of questions, all of which were still unanswerable.

The auburn–haired, hazel–eyed Jane could supply only two tiny fragments from her past. She remembered the name Captain Kirk and the city of Bath, Maine.

Bath was 150 miles from the bridge that spans the Merrimack River in Manchester, New Hampshire, where the woman had slipped on icy pavement and struck her head the night before.

Captain Kirk, on the other hand, could not be located as easily. To those trying to help the woman, the name conjured up a man light years away on some remote "Star Trek" planet.

The Bath Police Department was contacted. There had been no report of a missing person fitting her description. Captain Kirk was easier to find than previously anticipated, however. He was an officer with The Salvation Army in Bath.

The Manchester police called me at 7:00 that Saturday morning. Soon I was standing beside Jane's bed, located in the hospital hallway and surrounded by curtains. "I'm Captain Forster," I said, extending my hand. The woman's grip and the expression on her face were both asking for answers.

"I'm from The Salvation Army," I said. After a moment's pause, which seemed much longer, I asked, "Do you know about the Army?"

She searched the darkened closets of her mind, then said, "No. I don't think so."

I considered asking her some other questions, but I could see that her energy had already been drained by police inquiries. A tear trickled down her cheek, and she didn't brush it away. Perhaps she was hoping that I wouldn't notice.

"Someone must be looking for me," she said. "There must be a family that I belong to." Her wedding ring suggested this was true.

I had hoped that my Salvation Army uniform would bring a flicker of recognition, but my assumption that she was a Salvationist was wrong. A phone call to Captain Kirk brought me no closer to a solution. Neither he nor his wife knew the woman I described.

The hospital cafeteria was empty. I had oatmeal with brown sugar and deep thoughts. What is it like to wonder who you are? How would I feel if my wife had an accident and no one knew who she was? I was resolved to help Jane Doe find her real identity. "Lord," I prayed, "help me put together the pieces of Jane's life which have been cut up by an amnesia jigsaw. Lead me to the people she loves."

"A gift," she said, as I came back to her bedside. It was my turn to wear a confused expression. "My family got a thank–you card from someone in Bath, Maine, for a Christmas gift that we gave them," she said, excited over this new clue. "I remember the postmark on the envelope. Will this help?"

"I'm sure it will," I said. My heart didn't hold the confidence of my words. "Let's pray that it will." I held her hand as we prayed.

A young woman from Manchester was working with The Salvation Army in Bath. She might prove to be our link. Although I learned that the woman had gone to Portland for the day, I was given a number where she could be reached. After two phone calls and lengthy delays, I spoke to her and explained our dilemma. Her only guess was that Jane might be a woman she used to work with in a Manchester laundry. She gave me the name of another woman who had worked there with them. At my request the woman agreed to come to the hospital to identify Jane Doe.

My excitement and joy nearly turned to despair when she told me, "I've never seen this woman in my life."

The woman from the laundry gave me the name of another woman who had been friendly with Valerie, the girl from Bath. She had never met the woman, but she knew that Valerie had been friendly with their family.

The woman was sick with the flu. She knew Valerie but had no idea who Jane Doe might be.

I was supposed to be home by noon for my daughter's birthday party. It was now 12:25. I knew I wouldn't be able to settle into the party atmosphere, and I also knew that my eleven–year–old daughter and my wife were very understanding. I just couldn't relax until Jane recovered her name.

I called Valerie in Portland again. She was anxious to solve the mystery, but she didn't have any other ideas. I had thought of one.

"Do you have an address book in your purse?" I asked.

"Yes," she said. "Why?"

"Please thumb through it and give me the names of anyone who might resemble Jane's description, even remotely."

"I don't know if it will do any good, but I'll try," she said. She gave me six names, but she had little or no confidence in any of them.

"Have you gotten all the way through the address book?" I asked.

She gave me one final name from the back of her book, but she didn't think that it would be the woman we were looking for because she had had no contact with her for over a year.

I was immediately on the phone, making my way through the list. Each time someone answered the phone, I'd breathe a sigh of relief and explain my reason for calling. All were sympathetic, but none could offer any further clues.

One place I called had been disconnected; another one didn't answer. The next–to–last call I made rang a long time, and I finally had to hang up without an answer. I decided then that if the last call wasn't the connection I needed, I would have to track down the disconnect and the two no answers that I had received.

I prayed, "Lord, let this be the one."

A teenaged girl answered the phone. I introduced myself, then asked, "Is your mom at home?"

"No, she isn't," the girl said.

"Do you know where she is?" I asked.

"No, we don't," she said with a trembling voice.

I paused before I asked the next question, "Did your mom come home last night?" I asked finally.

The girl was near tears. "No, she didn't. We thought that she went to visit a friend, but none of her friends know where she is." She began to weep.

"Your mom is okay," I said. "Tell your dad to meet me at the Medical Center in twenty minutes. He will know me by my Salvation Army uniform."

When we walked into the hospital room, Jane looked directly at me. She didn't seem to know her husband at all.

He reached for her and she pulled back and screamed. Patiently, he took her hand and patted it slowly. She became calmer. The silence continued for several minutes as the attending nurse and I watched and waited for something to happen.

Suddenly the woman burst into tears and reached out to embrace her husband. The light had returned to her darkened memory. The Jane Doe wristband could be discarded. She was back in the arms of someone she loved.

The nurse and I left the room quietly. We spent a few moments in the hallway praising God and rejoicing over one who had been lost, but now was found.

Major Ed Forster

Where Earth and Sky Are One

Jill lay listening to the sounds of the night, the quiet breathing of Helen, her roommate, the slightly louder breathing of Helen's dog, Vep, and her own dog, Bee. From outside came the hypnotic drone of crickets announcing that the world must surely be theirs by way of sheer numbers. From the nearby kennel a dog barked twice, and then once again the world was given over to the crickets and the sleepers.

She felt the hands of her Braille watch. It was a quarter past one. The drapes moved out from the window at the hand of a passing breeze, letting in the smell of the September night.

She closed her eyes, and she could see the stars as she was sure they must look. It had been two long years since she had seen anything with her physical eyes, but she could remember every detail of the soft blue in the night sky.

A plane, flying high, momentarily broke the night quiet, and in her imagination she rose and flew with it, enjoying the endless beauty of the evening. In Jill's mind there lived two kinds of people: those she secretly called the *sky people*—her mother and father, her friends at school, the trainers here at Guiding Eyes for the Blind—all those who could see. All other blind people, including herself, she called the *earth people*. She felt that the earth people were like a giant plane with no motor, bound forever to the ground in their world of darkness.

Jill knew she was feeling sorry for herself, but she couldn't help it. She was seventeen, about to enter her senior year in high school, and she was blind.

Sure, she knew there were things worse, a lot worse, but that knowledge didn't help much. The kids at school had been great after the automobile accident, and sometimes she could almost believe that it didn't matter to them that she couldn't see; but always there was that barrier between earth and sky.

She knew, too, that she had been lucky to continue going to public school and not the school for the blind. She had been able to get a scanner and screen–reading software for her computer in addition to recorded versions of almost all her books. And there had always been volunteers who were more than glad to read for her.

"God has been good to provide all these things for you," her mother would say, and Jill supposed she was right, but in a far corner of her mind lurked the thought, "How can He be good, really good, and take the beauty and freedom out of my world?"

For not only did the sky people live in a world of beauty, but also a world of freedom. How could she feel free, groping her way along with a cane or holding on to someone's arm? Oh, how she longed to be able to go wherever she wished, whenever she wished! It had been a small thought—she dared not even hope—of freedom which had prompted her to apply to Guiding Eyes for the Blind for a guide dog.

Her mother had been overjoyed when a representative of the school had called to say that Jill had been accepted for the twenty–six–day training period with a dog. As usual, her mother had said, "God is so good."

Jill supposed that part of her problem in failing to see God's good-ness was that, unlike the sky, she could no longer see God in her mind's eye. She had long ago lost her adolescent image of God—a sort of combination of Howard Hughes and Buddha, mysterious, all powerful, but somehow comfortable and chubby. It was hard to attrib-ute goodness, especially in its compromised forms, when there was no one she envisioned to attribute it to. Even the wonderful prospect of reclaimed freedom with her guide dog was, in her way of thinking, a compromised version of freedom.

The videos and magazine articles she had read about owning a guide dog had been made of mainly sentiment. There was no mention of the tediousness of working with a dog in the heat and the rain for hours, trying to learn just the basics of walking, stopping, sitting at desks, crossing streets, climbing into cars, catching buses, or eating in restaurants. It all seemed to reinforce only the earth–bound barriers.

"See you a minute, Jill?" Hank, the trainer in charge of her class, had asked that evening after dinner. "I was wondering if anything is bothering you."

"No, why?"

"I think you know why, Jill. Your work with Bee is almost perfect, you know that, but I don't think you're happy. Perhaps *happy* is the wrong word—maybe *pleased* is more what I mean. Don't you like Bee?"

"Sure, I guess so," Jill said quickly. "I'd never thought much about it. She takes me where I want to go."

Hank took a moment before he spoke. "Jill, a dog is more than a cane. You can't just use her, there's got to be feeling. I'm going to ask you something. Do you really want a dog? And if you do, are you willing to give as well as take? Giving is more than just caring for her—it's caring about her. It's not just saying 'good dog' at the right time—it's saying those words with—well, love.

"I have a feeling that you came here expecting a dog to perform some sort of miracle and give you back your sight, but it just doesn't work that way. She'll give you her eyes—but you need to do the *seeing;* and believe me, a lot of times seeing has nothing to do with the eyes.

"I'd like to see you finish the training, Jill, and take Bee home with you—but only if you want to. So, you decide between now and the end of the week. Remember, you're not doing this for your mother or for me or anybody else—just yourself. Keep this in mind: A guide dog used with love and understanding can give you what amounts to unlimited freedom, but one used mechanically can be just another symbol of your blindness."

Lying there listening to the night, Jill knew that Hank was right, and she knew something else—she didn't have any feeling for the dog. It was as though the same barrier that separated earth from sky also separated her from Bee.

Was the real truth that she could no longer exist on the same level with anyone or anything that could see?

Jill lived in a state of tension all the next day. That evening they were to have their first and only night class, and she decided that afterward she would tell Hank that she wanted to go home as soon as it could be arranged. She felt that she would never be able to communicate with that sixty–five pounds of Labrador retriever who was supposed to substitute for her sight.

As usual, the two classes of six traveled by van to the nearby town of Peekskill, where the outdoor training was done. She knew that the route they were to follow had been given in detail, but she just hadn't been able to concentrate.

"Jill and Helen," Hank called to them after everyone was ready and standing with their dogs on the sidewalk. "You gals understand everything?"

"Sure," Helen said, and Jill nodded.

"Good. Okay, pick up your harnesses and have fun."

There was something exciting about traveling alone at night, and in spite of her determination to go home she found herself enjoying the experience. Of course, she knew they weren't really alone. Hank was always watching a short distance away, but unless they encountered serious trouble they were left strictly on their own.

Jill and Helen made two crossings, each taking her turn in the lead. They walked another block and, as always, stopped at the curb.

"It's my turn to cross first this time, isn't it?" Jill asked.

"We don't cross this street," Helen said, "We make a right turn."

"No, we don't," Jill said, although in fact she didn't know. Somehow she just felt that she wanted to argue.

"No, Jill," Helen said. "Remember, this is route two, and we . . ."

"I don't care," Jill interrupted, "I'm going to cross." She gave Bee the command "forward."

They hadn't gone far when suddenly Bee hesitated as though she was unsure. Then Jill felt someone grab her arm and try to pull her shoulder bag free.

Jill's reaction was pure instinct. Quickly she turned to face her assailant and brought up her knee hard.

"Bee, forward, hup–up," she said as the man let go of her. Bee responded at once to the command, and together they ran.

She had been running for about half a block when she heard a breathless shout. "Hey, wait for me!" It was Hank.

She stopped and dropped to her knees, her arms hugging the panting Bee. "Good girl," she said. "Good girl!"

"You okay?" Hank asked coming up beside them. "Sorry I didn't get to you sooner. I'd just gone around the corner to tell Helen to stop when it happened. The police are after him now. Hope nothing like this'll ever happen to you again, but purse–snatchers are a part of life. You sure knew what to do. Lady, you were moving like you could see!"

"I think I'm beginning to," Jill said quietly as she stroked Bee's floppy ears.

"Good," he said sharply. "Now I hope you can *listen* the next time I explain a route!" But along with the sharpness she heard a note of understanding.

"Please fasten your seatbelts," the flight attendant said, and Jill tugged hers together. Bee had already fallen asleep at her feet. They were on their way home to begin the adventure of their life together.

Jill had done a lot of thinking since that night a week ago when, for the first time in over two years, she had been able to "run free." She had acted on her own in an emergency, and Bee had supplied the needed sight. Somehow it had not seemed like a compromise at all.

She had been so busy erecting a barrier between herself and those who could see that she had forgotten her own part in the scheme of things. She had been so intent on wishing for the sky that she had failed to see the horizon where earth and sky became one.

She had resented God for taking away her sight, without stopping to think that the loss was far less tragic than she made it seem. God had left her memories of beauty, and no matter how much things might change, those memories would always be hers.

He had given her the means to finish school with the rest of her class, and now with Bee she had an ever–present pair of willing eyes.

More importantly, Jill could see God again—through the love of her mother and father, through the help of her friends, in the patience and understanding of Hank and all the others at Guiding Eyes, and in the loyalty of Bee. Surely all these were the spiritual image of God Himself.

As the plane lifted from the runway and climbed toward the sky, Jill's thoughts flew, as well, toward an exciting and challenging future.

Phyllis Campbell

His Windows Opened to the Sky

Colonel Raymond Robbins was one of the most remarkable figures in American history whose influence extended into politics, social service and international affairs; but his name is forgotten now except by a few who lived through the stirring days of World War I and the years of tension which followed.

A public figure for more than forty years, Colonel Robbins had many friends—and possibly as many enemies, for he loved to support unpopular causes. When a spinal injury took him out of the public eye, he continued with correspondences that circled the globe. In winter, he entertained diplomats, politicians, churchmen, social workers and writers in his home near Brooksville, Florida. They came to talk, to argue—and sometimes to agree.

Raymond Robbins had been an orphan who lived with relatives in an old house that dated back to Florida's pioneer days. Treated kindly but impersonally, he longed for something of his own, a family who loved him, land that he could till—his own land, with pine woods and a view of the valley. He dreamed of owning the farm on which he worked and lived, but it was many years before his dream came true.

He was not yet twenty–one when he set out to seek his fortune. Strong and willing to work, he tackled each job he found. One night he joined a group of men heading for the fabulous Klondike gold rush. On this journey he saw men lose their temper and sometimes their sanity in the lust for gold. There were bloody fights, and many who started never lived to see the end of the trail.

One night along that trail Robbins lay in his sleeping bag, too tired to sleep, wondering how he had ever come so far from home. Next to him was a young man, the only one in the group who had showed no irritation or resentment.

"What keeps you so calm and cheerful?" Robbins asked him.

The fellow thought for a moment then answered, "I guess it's religion."

"Religion!" said Robbins incredulously. "I know plenty of people who have religion, but they don't act like you. There must be something else. What's your secret?"

"That's all there is," replied his companion. "Just plain religion. If you get real religion, it will keep you in all kinds of places."

Robbins pondered the matter. He had been reared in a nominally religious home, but never before had he known anyone who seemed to really "have religion." Was there really a power in faith that could keep one steady, could change a man's nature, turn him around and start him out in a new direction?

The next day they found their way to the goldfields; the question was forgotten in the mad rush to stake a claim. Robbins was one of the few who made a strike, and his newfound riches filled his mind to the exclusion of anything else.

When the excitement cooled and his mine was being worked, he remembered the conversation of that night. He never saw or heard from the young man again, but the seed that was planted would continue to grow—and that was the first of the four vistas that opened to God for Raymond Robbins.

Months later in the wildest part of the Klondike, Robbins and his companions stopped for the night at a small Roman Catholic mission. For the first time in months he slept between sheets and ate good food. He learned that the fur–clad missionary residing there was a university graduate and trained to be a lawyer, but he had given up a promising future to enter the priesthood and spend his life among the indigenous people of the Northwest.

"What's the use?" asked Robbins. "You admit that education only makes these people more susceptible to the frustrations that our more 'civilized' societies face. You say you've made only a few converts in twenty–five years. Why do you go on?"

Smiling, the priest replied, "I agree that it might seem hopeless, but it will not be in vain. Nothing done for God is. You think in terms of a few years; God thinks in millenniums, and His Church must think that way also."

The way, thought Robbins, was a little clearer now. He was not to judge religion by the least satisfactory followers of Christ but by the most. He had met two men for whom religion worked; perhaps there were more. The second window had opened to the west, where toward their sunset went a dying people, comforted and strengthened by the minister of God's mercy. The priest had shown Robbins the path of duty in the face of hardship.

Months went by and the long trail toward riches was behind him. Independently wealthy yet not satisfied just to live a life of luxury, Robbins traveled again. One night, he and a friend became lost in the wilderness. Food was soon gone and snow buried the trail. They made camps for the night. Snow–blind and weak from fever, his companion slept as Robbins felt the numbness creeping over his own body. It would be an easy way to go, he thought, just to sleep and not wake up. Someone had said that when you began to dream of a warm, sunny day, your sleep would no longer be interrupted.

Robbins began to dream of the old home place beneath a sunny sky, corn tassels ripening in the field, the blue of the lake. So peaceful, so warm and pleasant.

Then a sudden shift of the wind—or something else, he never knew what—awakened him to his danger. Staggering to his feet, he made his way over to where his partner lay. He was scarcely breathing, and Robbins knew that it would be only a short time before he would freeze to death. He shook the icy figure. "Wake up!" he cried, and getting no response he began to slap the man's face.

Suddenly his friend awoke and, in his blindness and delirium, concluded that he was being attacked by an enemy! Lunging to his feet, he reached for his knife. Robbins turned and fled, stumbling and falling in the snow, but managing to keep ahead of the maddened man.

Finally exertion brought the return of sanity to his friend as he sank to the ground and thanked Robbins for saving his life.

"Stay here," Robbins said, "and I will try to find the way." Peering through the darkness, he headed in what he hoped was the right direction. He tried to pray, but the words would not come. Then he saw an incredible sight.

Standing upright in the snow was a cross. He moved closer and put out his hand. It was no hallucination, for the cross stood firm. It marked the grave of someone who had died, perhaps long ago.

Here was his answer—not a miracle, but the fact of death in the midst of life. That cross upraised against the Yukon sky was the symbol of life and death and immortality. For Raymond Robbins, that night the third window opened to the sky.

He and his companion found the path that led to the next settlement, and life went on.

Three windows had opened, yet the way was not clear. It remained for a young woman in a Congregational mission, months later, to open the window to the east and let the sun come in. Giving him a copy of the New Testament, she spoke of faith and joy in service. In his room one night, he took the book and began to read. In the seventh chapter of John's Gospel he found these words: *If anyone chooses to do God's will, he will find out whether my teaching comes from God or whether I speak on my own.*

Perhaps his trouble had been that he had tried to reason everything out. Why not, instead, try to do God's will and then wait for the understanding to come later?

Kneeling beside his bed, Raymond Robbins prayed. Whatever God wanted him to do he would do, even if it meant giving up his fortune. As he prayed, all of his speculations were swallowed up in a cry of affirmation, "Lord, reveal Your will!" There was no ecstasy, no vision. He then calmly went to sleep and left the future to God.

Not long afterward, he went to see the head of the Congregational mission. "I want to help," he said. The bewildered minister looked at the rough clothing that Robbins still wore and shook his head.

But Robbins was not to be rebuffed. Taking five hundred dollars from his pocket, he laid it on the table between them. "As a pledge of good faith, if I cause you any trouble or do any damage, this will pay for it." Convinced of Robbins' sincerity, the minister consented to give him a trial.

I first met Colonel Raymond Robbins in 1944—on a mild November day when he told me that story of his life. I had come to do an interview, but I was given more than what I had asked.

Through a tall window in the old house where he was raised and later lived his final days, I could see acres of orange groves beyond the woods. As he talked, I noticed that Colonel Robbins' eyes seldom looked away from that narrowing vista between the trees.

Noticing my interest, he smiled and said, "That is only one vista. When you leave, ask my secretary to show you the other three. Each one leads somewhere and each one starts here. A man has to start somewhere, but no matter where he starts, he comes eventually to the same place."

When the interview was over, I thanked Colonel Robbins for his story and asked permission to publish it.

Frowning thoughtfully, he looked out the window again. "No," he said, "not now, please. The road may not be long ahead of me, but I would prefer that you wait until I come to the end of it. When I am gone, you can make any use of it you care to."

As I turned to leave, Colonel Robbins left his view from the window to face me for a moment. "You are a young minister," he said, "and you have your future before you. Let me tell you this—the world wants the gospel; the world must have God. I have failed many times since I first found Him, but I have not stopped trying to do His will, and as I followed His direction, I learned of His doctrine."

I thanked him again and began my walk around the grounds of Chinsegut Hill. From each side of the house there was a vista—to the south, the west, the north and east—each one cutting clearly through the trees, each one seeming, at the end, to touch the sky.

Now I understood the connection between each view and the story of his life.

Colonel Robbins died a few years later, after I had left Florida, and the story he told me that day was never released for publication until now. The other day, as I looked through some old papers in my files, I found it and reread it for the first time in many years. I suppose now he wouldn't mind that you have read it, too.

R. P. Marshall

By Way of the Water Tank

The Muslim call to prayer echoed off the courtyard walls, an ancient sound, as familiar to the ears of its people as the heat from Pakistan's merciless sun is to the clay–earthen country that bakes beneath it.

Phil made a face at the noise. Once the sound had sent chills coursing through his body, but now he could barely remember how *cold* felt. From the shadows of the veranda, Phil's uncle, David Hastings, strode briskly to silence the water pump—a gesture of understanding toward his neighbors and their beliefs. Why should their prayers to Allah be interrupted by the *thud–thump–thud* of a pump drawing precious water into the mission's holding tank?

Phil, however, thought the townspeople deserved to be annoyed by the engine. After all, the mission residents had been denied the use of the village well. Evidently the spring would be considered "polluted" if a Christian took from it a cup of water.

"I sure wish their prayers didn't interfere with Aunt Mary's dish-washing," Phil muttered. "The engine restarts so hard."

"Your aunt might also rearrange her mealtimes." Uncle David wiped his face. Even after six months, the daily 115–degree heat bore heavily upon him. "If we think they're stubborn, what must they think of us? No one else eats dinner before night cools the ground."

"Go on inside, if you want," Phil offered. "I'll fight the flywheel."

As soon as the call to prayer was finished, the water had to rise again. In this country one slept soundly in the knowledge that the tank was filled to meet the morning's needs.

"Are you sure I should leave you out here alone?" Uncle David seemed doubtful. When an adult worked on the water pump engine, the boys of the town pegged stones over the wall; when it was Phil in the center of the compound, the pebbles changed to rocks.

Unconsciously Phil raised his hand to touch the bandage on the back of his neck. Usually the missiles only bruised, but that one had been razor sharp. "I know who threw it," Phil remarked softly. "If I were at home, I would have gotten even before now."

His uncle's dry chuckle reminded him that home was a half–world away. And in the back bedroom of that house, Cousin Jeff was dozing in those final moments before the alarm went off. Jeff was the boy who should have been here. He would have met the calls to prayer and the stones with understanding and patience. Jeff knew how to face disappointment and pain. But he wasn't here.

Phil hadn't figured he could come near to Jeff's example. All he knew was that, with the required wheelchair, walker, and other devices for Jeff's recuperation, there wasn't room in the house for two boys. So while he couldn't share his aunt and uncle's enthusiasm for the mission field, he, at least, matched their determination to go.

As Phil reached the structure that centered the enclosure, he heard whispers on the far side of the wall. His quick fingers opened switches and made adjustments. Anticipated pain would be forgotten as soon as the flywheel demanded his total attention.

This night the engine caught hold with surprising willingness. Its first protesting grunts and puffs of grey smoke vanished quickly, and the regular rhythmic drumming sound started just as a rock the size of a grapefruit dropped near his foot.

"Sorry about that, Ashid!" Phil's Urdu jibe rose above the engine's drone. "Your aim is poor tonight. About six inches off target." An angry torrent of native tongue flew back at him, accompanied by more rocks. Phil escaped to the veranda, threw back his head and laughed.

"The size of their rocks grows along with my command of their language," Phil reported to his aunt and uncle. "Maybe it's just as well they won't converse with me. I'd rather be ignored altogether."

"Those who ignore may never hear, I think." Aunt Mary shook her head. "The boys who throw rocks at least have realized we are different. The Apostle Paul was an authority on thrown rocks, and think of how he spread the gospel."

The room's single overhead light flickered, pulsed and dimmed once more. Phil glared at the ceiling.

"Paul didn't have people trying to short out his electrical system. How many times has that happened now?"

"I'd better order more wire." Uncle David shrugged.

"The people are probably a bit envious of the electricity in our home," Aunt Mary suggested. "No one else has it except the government officials. Otherwise, power goes only to the public buildings, the school and the hospital."

"Plus the mosque," Phil added, "to drive the amplifiers for those hideous wails at prayer time."

"I enjoy hearing the *muezzin's* call." His uncle smiled. "It reminds me that God hears prayers anytime."

"The lights and the refrigerator may interest the people," Phil admitted to his aunt, "but the pump and water tank really draw their attention. Every day the camels all have their loads shifted outside our open gate. The goatherds are reassembled there, too. But the drovers only look. No one speaks."

"One day they will." Uncle David's voice lost its weariness. "The Scriptures are filled with lives that were changed at watering places."

Phil turned his palms up and frowned at the callouses. If souls could be won by sinking water pipes, he had made his contribution. And if not, he was grateful just to be able to bathe away the dirt.

The next morning Phil warily undertook the well–worn trip from the mission's wall, through the old village, to the recently constructed government square beyond to post the weekly dispatches. This made him an open target, but his school assignments needed to go out by the morning's mail.

During the mornings, most of the Pakistani children were closed away in the village school, becoming their country's literate citizens of tomorrow, but Ashid and his friends seemed old enough to be beyond compulsory attendance. Phil's feet churned up dust as he wondered what occupied a young Pakistani's days between the age of graduation and the age of marriage to a bride of his family's choosing.

His walk always took him near the town well, the social center of the village. Women, covered from head to toe in suffocating *burkas* which hid them in public, crowded around the brick structure.

How they could recognize each other when wearing those tent–like garments, Phil couldn't figure. Yet they chatted as they worked, reminding him of his mother's friends at the supermarket back home. Usually he could sense their curious stares resting upon him even though their eyes were covered by a window of mesh.

Today, however, their attention strayed toward the far shadows. There was movement of indistinct white, green and red. Then Phil could identify the faces of the teenaged pack moving out from the shadows to bar his way.

"Eh, Christian! You no longer have the courage of your walls."

Ashid was leader and spokesman, his tan face contorted into a smirk. He spoke halting English, but the threat was apparent in his posture. Both hands were open, fingers rigidly extended from bent elbows nestled waist–high.

"I need no walls. Jesus Christ stands with me." Phil, surprised at how easily the Urdu phrases came to mind, called back softly.

"And will this Jesus Christ swim with you? If so, He also will drown in the well." Ashid lapsed into his own tongue.

Although the boys had circled him and were forcing him toward the water, Phil had to smile. It was the first time that a non–Christian had spoken directly to him.

"But that cannot be." Phil felt rough mortar scratch against his legs. "Your well will be poisoned if a Christian merely drinks from it. Your leaders have said so. If a Christian were to drown in it, the whole town must die of thirst."

Their guard relaxed as the boys considered the disaster that could threaten their lives. Phil took advantage of their doubt to walk through the ring. The shadows, only a short dash away, seemed to promise safety. Instead, Phil walked slowly along the sunlit street. He supposed that his attackers were already bending to scoop up weapons.

"Today you will not swim, Christian dog!" Ashid's voice swelled.

"But only because this drought has already dried up the other wells. Instead, we will make you run."

The rocks showered around Phil. He plodded on, keeping his steps slow. One stone glanced off his sleeve. Another thumped his back. As he moved nearer the mission wall, the blows seemed lighter. It was as if the gang no longer had their hearts in the skirmish.

"Any news from town?" Uncle David patted the water pump engine before wiping oil from his hands.

"I hear some of the farm wells have dried up," Phil volunteered. He couldn't mention the confrontation with Ashid and his friends.

"And all the riverbeds look like roadways," Uncle David spoke grimly, glancing up at the cloudless sky. "The farmers must carry water from the town well. Many of their animals are already dead. Now I fear for the people. Our well is drilled and pierces deep, but the town well only caps an underground stream."

"Couldn't these people ask us for water?" Phil asked in frustration. Uncle David shook his head thoughtfully. "I pray that they will."

The next time Phil went to the dispatch office, the women no longer lingered at the town well. From the way they carried their clay jugs, Phil could tell the containers were only partly filled.

Then one morning he pushed open the courtyard gates and blinked. David Hastings' prayer had been answered. No one was near, but five jugs of baked clay were lined up outside the wall.

Phil grabbed two, carried them to the storage tank and opened the tap. He lugged the pair back and lifted another set. On his return, the full jugs were gone. An empty one sat there, instead.

Uncle David came to the doorway of the house, caught hold of the situation and reacted quickly. He called to Aunt Mary and soon the three of them were moving from gate to water tank and back again.

Turning quickly, Phil would see figures dart forward to retrieve the water. As he passed his aunt, Phil exchanged a smile with her. He was picturing the people being happily surprised the next day when the water hadn't made them sick. Perhaps tomorrow would find them more trusting, he thought, and ready to lift their own loads.

But today, as the sun's intensity increased, so did the length of the line of water jugs. Finally Aunt Mary staggered under her burden. Uncle David hurried to her and led her to the shade. Phil continued his effort undauntedly, knowing that he and the mission pump were making no headway in the race against the clay containers.

Then he heard a familiar voice. "Get into the shade before the sun burns you to an ash. I will fill and carry for a while." Through squinted lids, Phil recognized Ashid's smirking grin. No energy left within him to react, he walked slowly to the porch and collapsed.

Later another boy came, spoke to Ashid, and took over at the tap. Ashid moved slowly across the courtyard.

"The sun is hard, even for a Pakistani," he admitted, squatting next to Phil. "Water is our only defense against it."

"What you need is the living water. If a man drinks of it, he will never be thirsty again." Phil didn't look at Ashid. Instead he watched another boy step hesitantly into the compound.

"That's stupid!" Ashid snapped. "Everyone gets thirsty. Why say such a dumb thing?"

"Jesus said it, in the Bible," Phil grinned. "I can show you."

"I don't read English," Ashid shot back. "You could open the book and read anything. I couldn't tell the difference."

"Then read it in *your* language," Phil challenged. "I'll bring it."

Ashid looked surprised and skeptical as he waited. Because the teenagers already questioned why Allah refused to hear their prayers if they spoke in Urdu, not in Arabic, and why the *Qur'an* was considered holy only when written in Arabic, Uncle David had thought to provide the mission with Bibles in Urdu.

Ashid took the Book and frowned as he examined the page where Phil was pointing. He read the words, marked the place with a finger, and flipped to another page. Then he returned to the first verses and read them again—this time the frown had gone.

"This man understands about us, doesn't he?" Ashid asked, his head shaking in amazement.

"Of course He does. He is God's own Son," Phil answered. "Why don't you read more?"

"I must go back and help."

Ashid closed the Bible and handed it to Phil. "Zayd will come and rest now. You tell him about the special water, too. And then the others. I will send them, and you will show them the book."

Filled with an energy that no sun could burn away, Phil promised his new friend, "I will."

Marilyn Jakes Church

Capture of the White Swan

In the first decade of twentieth–century England, everybody on the west side of Birmingham knew Bertha Brooks. She and her husband Fred kept the White Swan public house on Barker Street. Perhaps it would be more accurate to say that she kept the bar with a steely eye on her customers, while Fred discreetly kept out of her way.

Bertha was a big woman, almost six feet in height and solidly built. Any guest of hers who drank too much and made himself a nuisance was to be pitied. She could pick up a man bodily and throw him through the swinging doors onto the sidewalk. When she stood behind the bar, her word was law to everyone under the grimy rafters. More than one sturdy ironworker had cause to regret disputing her decrees.

But for Bertha, life was full of trials. Every night Fred had to lie awake, knowing better than to doze off, while she recounted the misfortunes of the day. The delivery from the brewery had been late. The charwoman had not come to clean up. Somebody had slipped out without paying for his beer. To all her lamentations, Fred meekly replied, "Yes, my pet. I know it's 'ard. But maybe things'll mend."

Bertha had been in charge of the White Swan for five years when Susie Green came in one Saturday evening with a tambourine and a bundle of papers. Outside on the street Captain Denham and his soldiers of the Queen Street corps were holding an open air meeting. The captain, newly assigned to Birmingham, was a firm believer in laying siege with spiritual "blood and fire" to the strongholds of sin. In his opinion there was only one thing to do with a pub, and that was to attack it.

Susie was young and pretty. Light brown curls escaped from the corners of her Army bonnet as she walked straight to the bar and surveyed with clear blue eyes Bertha's strapping figure.

"The Salvation Army would like to help you and your customers," she said. "It prints this paper, *The War Cry,* every week to teach people about the love of God. The copies are only a penny each. How many do you want?"

Bertha's mouth fell open. She had never met anything like this before. If the proposition had come from a man, she would have rolled up her sleeves and pointed grimly to the door. But the sweet face and unwavering eyes disarmed her. What could she say to such a lovely child? Certainly nothing in bar room language.

The sweet face smiled at her, and the last bit of hostility in Bertha's heart became soft putty. She reached across the bar and took a *War Cry.*

"Why, luv," she said, managing a smile in return, "it's pleased I am to see you. The way you came in 'ere, you were just like a ray o' sunshine. Now what were you sayin' about this paper?"

"It's *The War Cry,*" Susie repeated, "and it does everybody good who reads it."

"Can it show people 'ow to get away from their troubles?"

"Yes, it can." Susie looked directly into Bertha's eyes. "It tells you how you can forget your troubles and enjoy a wonderful life with the Lord."

"I'll take three of 'em," Bertha said, dropping a three penny piece into Susie's tambourine, " 'cause nobody 'as more troubles than me."

A young fellow sidled up to the bar, a cigarette dangling loosely from his lips. He leered at Susie.

"Well, well!" he bantered. "Wot 'ave we 'ere?"

Bertha's glare instantly froze him in his tracks. "You 'ave me 'ere, Jim Coggins, and don't you forget it. Now give this lass a penny and take one o' them papers to read. A chap like you certainly needs 'elp."

Hurriedly Jim parted with his penny and escaped to a rear bench in the smoke room. Bertha threw a reassuring smile at Susie and then rapped loudly on the counter of the bar with a bottle. As if on command, the hubbub of voices at the tables subsided.

"Listen to me, you chaps," Bertha announced. "We 'ave a visit tonight from a Salvation Army lass. She's got some papers that'll do you a lot o' good. They're a penny apiece. I expect all my friends to buy one."

Evidently the invitation had enough significance to stir the men into action. For the next few minutes Susie was kept busy handing out papers and listening to the clink of coins in her tambourine.

When a laggard came under Bertha's watchful eye, she promptly routed him from his seat with scathing words. "What's the matter with you, Mike? 'Aven't you ever learned to read? And you, Tom? At least you can take one 'ome for the missus."

When the last *War Cry* had been sold, Susie turned gratefully to Bertha. "That was nice of you," she said. "We'll pray for you in our meetings."

"Well, luv." Bertha seemed doubtful. "I don't know as I need any prayers."

"Of course you do," smiled Susie. "Your troubles, you know. We'll ask the Lord to get at the root of them."

"Oh, yes, my troubles," Bertha agreed. "That's funny. I forgot all about 'em while I was talkin' to you. You will come and see me again, won't you?"

"I promise," Susie said.

Passing through the swinging doors of the White Swan, Susie went into the street. She nodded cheerfully to Captain Denham, who was waiting for her on the sidewalk with some anxiety.

"Here, Captain," she said, handing him the well–loaded tambourine. "With a bit of persistence and plenty of copies of *The War Cry,* I think we can take this place for the Lord."

During the following weeks Captain Denham conducted several open air meetings on Barker Street, and on each occasion Susie went into the White Swan with her bundle of papers. At her entrance Bertha would confide to her husband, " 'Ere comes the only bit o' sunshine in my life." Then she would announce to her customers, "The Army lass 'as come, chaps. Get your money ready."

But Susie was determined to do more than sell *The War Cry*. She had been praying earnestly for Bertha, asking God for guidance in dealing with her. Soon she began to see answers to her prayers.

During one of Susie's visits to the White Swan, Bertha expressed an interest in Susie's tambourine.

"I use it to make joyful noise to the Lord," Susie explained. "I tap it and shake it. Let me show you."

Without waiting for permission, Susie shook her tambourine and sang "When the Roll Is Called Up Yonder" to Bertha and her astonished customers. When she concluded, there was absolute silence in the room. Moments passed; then Bertha cleared her throat.

"What's this roll–callin' business all about?" she inquired.

"It means that God puts your name down in a book when you get saved," Susie said. "Then when you die, you're sure of a wonderful home in Heaven."

Brushing her hand across her eyes, Bertha quickly looked away and changed the subject.

"Well, luv, I wish I could sing as 'appily as you."

"It wouldn't take the Army long to teach you," Susie replied.

On another evening Bertha gazed admiringly at Susie's bonnet.

"Y'know," she speculated, "I think a 'at like that would suit me. If it doesn't cost more than ten shillings, maybe I could get one."

Susie shook her head. "You couldn't. Anybody who wears a hat like this has to be washed."

"What do you mean?" Indignation crept into Bertha's voice. "I use soap and water every mornin'."

"It isn't that kind of washing," said Susie with an engaging smile. "To wear this hat, you have to be washed in the 'Blood of the Lamb.' That cleanses you from sin and it also takes your troubles away."

"So 'at's the way to get rid o' my 'ardships," Bertha said. "I'll 'ave to think about it."

There was a chill wind accompanied by a bleak drizzle of rain on the Saturday night when Susie's prayers were completely answered. Some of Captain Denham's soldiers were dubious about the prospects of an open air meeting in such weather. But the captain set his jaw and called for a "stand to arms."

"Souls can be won for the Lord in all kinds of weather and in all kinds of places," he declared. He little knew the prophetic nature of his statement.

When Susie entered the White Swan, she found Bertha engaged in a heated argument with a customer. With a wary eye on the bottle in Bertha's hand, the man insisted he had been short–changed.

"I'm sure I gave you a shilling," he asserted.

"You gave me sixpence, and I gave you fourpence change," she snapped back at him. "Now get yourself through that door before I really lose my temper."

The man vanished, and Bertha turned a gloomy face toward Susie.

"Oh, luv," she sighed. "This 'as been a 'orrible day. Ever since I 'ad breakfast, nothin' 'as gone right. I never 'ad so many troubles."

A stream of compassion, warm and tender, flowed through Susie's heart. She walked to the other side of the bar and looked earnestly at Bertha. "Why don't you take all your cares to Jesus?" she said softly. "He's the only One who can wash them away and give you real peace."

Then, throwing her arms round Bertha's neck, she kissed her.

That was the moment when Bertha Brooks surrendered to the Army. She crumpled under Susie's kiss as Goliath did under David's pebble. Only Goliath never had the chance to kneel behind a bar and weep his heart out while a Salvationist led him to Christ.

Unable to believe the evidence of their eyes, the customers in the White Swan looked on in awed silence while Susie and Bertha wept and prayed together below the counter of the bar. It seemed that many minutes passed. Then Bertha rose to her feet. Her eyes were shining, and there was a strange radiance on her features.

" 'Ooray for Jesus!" she shouted. "My troubles are gone!"

From a back room where he had been working, her husband Fred came rushing into the bar. He gaped in astonishment at what he saw.

"Go and lie down, my pet," he gasped. "I'll get some medicine."

"Shut up," Bertha ordered. She turned to her customers. "Now I want everybody to listen to me. I've just made a decision. I want all o' you to get up and leave quietly. Right this minute the White Swan is closed—and closed for good."

A groan of protest came from the men on the benches, but Bertha simply rapped on the counter and pointed to the door. Slowly the men began to file out. Fred was a picture of anguish as he stared at the retreating figures.

"What'll we do now?" he muttered dismally. "No pub, no livin'."

"You'll go back to your bricklayin', Fred Brooks, that's what you'll do," Bertha said. "But first, I'm takin' you to that Salvation Army meetin' out yonder in the street. You're goin' to be washed just like I was. And what's more, I'll be standin' by to see that the Army gives you a good scrubbin.'"

Miserable and aghast, Fred considered his predicament. He had a strange feeling that the floor was rocking beneath his feet. Several times his mouth opened and closed as he groped for words. At last he found them.

"Yes, my pet."

Albert Hoy

Winter

Everything in time and under heaven

finally falls asleep;

Wrapped in blankets white, all creation

shivers underneath;

Still, I notice You when branches crack

And in my breath on frosted glass.

Even now in death, You open doors for life to enter.

A City of a Million Strangers

When they came out of the theater, Tess saw that it was snowing again. The rising wind whipped the snowflakes into a whirling tumult of whiteness. Her heart sank. It was going to be a nasty walk to the car parked four blocks away.

Raising her coat collar against the force of the gale, she glanced down at her nine–year–old son. "Button up your jacket, Jerry," she said. "Do you want to be frozen stiff by the time we get to the car?"

Her husband stood beside her, shaking his head in disbelief. "Man, I can't say as I'm crazy about the weather they have here in the wintertime. You and Jerry had better wait here, Tess, while I go and get the car."

She touched his arm. "Watch your step, Steve. Don't walk too fast. The sidewalks will be slippery."

As Steve started up the street, she grasped Jerry's hand, drawing him back toward the theater entrance.

How she hated all this cold and discomfort! But it seemed this was the kind of weather they should have expected in January in the midwest. How was she ever going to stand it?

The familiar longing swept over her again to be back in the small town in California, where she and Steve had lived most of their lives. They would be enjoying a mild winter now if Steve's company hadn't transferred him to this big city in the midwest two months ago.

Steve earned good money as an electronics engineer. *Only money isn't everything,* she thought. Not when you have to live thousands of miles from relatives and friends and make your home in a city you simply hated.

Jerry was tugging on her arm. "Come on, Mom. Dad's here. Let's hurry and get in the car."

Steve had the heater turned on, and it was wonderful to be greeted by the cozy warmth of the car. Still, Tess felt tense and nervous about driving in the storm. When the rear end of the car slid sideways against the curb when Steve turned a corner, she clutched his arm.

"Please be careful, Steve," she gasped. "Don't drive so fast."

"Take it easy, Tess," Steve returned. "You don't have to tell me how to drive. I've been doing it for fifteen years."

She sat on the edge of the seat peering through the windshield. "But you aren't used to driving in snow and ice. It would be dreadful if we got into an accident."

"Well, you're not helping matters any. Just sit back and relax—"

The car skidded again as he slowed for a traffic light. Her heart leaped into her throat. "Watch out!" she cried. "Oh, dear, this is awful. We never should have gone to a movie tonight."

Her husband glanced at her sharply. "It was your idea, if you remember. You were bored to death, you said, at being cooped up in that apartment all the time. You made it sound like a matter of life and death for you to go out this evening."

Yes, it was true. Only it wasn't just tonight she'd felt that way. She'd been bored and restless ever since they came here. Life was so different from what they had been used to.

Tess was so lonely at times it was like something eating away inside her. She saw people on the streets and in the supermarket where she shopped, but they passed her by, silent and withdrawn, each one busy with personal affairs. There wasn't a single friendly face among the hundreds she saw every day. She would never feel at home in this big, bustling city.

Suddenly her thoughts were interrupted as a fire engine came up behind them in the outside lane and roared past, its siren wailing. She exchanged a glance with her husband. When they looked off to the right they could see it—the flush of spreading crimson that lit up the night sky.

Fear had already begun to creep over Tess by the time they approached the apartment building where they lived. She saw the milling crowd and the three fire engines standing in the street.

Steve stopped the car, his face grim. "The fire appears to be on the south side of the building."

Jerry's eyes were round as saucers as they climbed from the car. "Gosh, it's a really big one!" he exclaimed. "And we had to be sitting in a dumb movie tonight. I'll bet we've missed half the excitement."

"Please hush, Jerry!" Tess snapped. "We have to find out exactly what has happened." She shuddered as she looked at the thick cloud of smoke billowing from the building.

Shoving their way through the mass of people standing around, they found a heavyset policeman blocking the street. They could feel the heat of the fire now.

"Sorry, folks, but you'll have to stay where you are," he ordered. "It's too dangerous to come any closer. Besides, we need room here for the firemen to move around."

"Please let us pass," Tess begged. "We live in that building."

"Hey, come here a minute!" The officer shouted over to an elderly man dressed in overalls. When he came forward, the policeman asked him, "Are these people tenants of yours?"

It was Mr. Finley, the superintendent of the building. He looked very upset. "I don't know how to tell you people this," he said, shaking his head. "Seems the fire started on the second floor next to your apartment. As you can see, they still haven't got it under control."

"Are you telling us we've lost everything?" Steve asked tersely.

Mr. Finley's eyes were sympathetic as he nodded his head. There was nothing else he could say.

"Oh, no!" Tess was hardly conscious that she had screamed the words aloud. She couldn't believe this was happening, yet it was all horribly true. They had lost everything in the apartment.

To make things worse, nothing was insured. The apartment was only a temporary home until they found a house they wanted to buy. They hadn't renewed the insurance policy on their personal effects, deciding to wait until they found a permanent place to settle before taking care of such matters. Now everything was gone.

A great wave of bitterness burned through Tess. She had never liked this awful city from the day they arrived. How she hated it now!

Suddenly she was aware that a small, gray–haired woman had her arms around her. "You poor things. I know how you must feel!" She gazed at Tess with pity. "I don't know what your plans are, but I'm going to insist that you come home with us tonight. We live in the next block."

The woman's name was Mrs. Tomlin, and her husband stood with her. In spite of their frail appearance and advanced years, they proved to be very capable people during those next few hours. Before Tess and her family knew what was happening, the three of them were being taken to the Tomlins' big, old–fashioned home, where Mrs. Tomlin served them coffee and homemade cupcakes.

Tess couldn't help thinking this was the first gesture of friendship anyone had shown them in the whole city since they had arrived—and now it just didn't seem to matter very much. She couldn't relax and enjoy it. Her whole body was encased in a strange numbness that made it impossible for her to feel anything.

They stayed with the Tomlins for a week while Steve scouted the neighborhood for a furnished house they could rent. Tess never went with him. Filled with despair, she wasn't interested where they lived now. Deep in her heart she was hoping he wouldn't be able to find a house. She didn't want to live in this cold, unfriendly city any longer.

"Why don't we go back home, Steve?" she asked one day. "Except for the Tomlins, who do we know here? I want to be where we have friends, people who care about us."

He stared at her unhappily. "This is where my work is now, Tess," he said. "And it's not going to do any good for you to continue brooding about this. What we have to do now is look ahead."

Her husband's words didn't change her feelings. It seemed that everything was so pointless. How could two people even begin to make a new home for themselves in a situation like theirs?

The Tomlins seemed to lead a quiet life that revolved mainly around their church. Tess was amazed at how often they went to church, not only on Sundays but several other times during the week. Once or twice Mrs. Tomlin had invited Steve and Tess to go with them, but Tess quickly refused. She hadn't been near a church in years, and she certainly had no desire to start attending one now. She had no faith in the goodness of God after what had happened to them.

The day they moved into the house Steve found for them, Tess did what was necessary to make it livable. She had no real interest in their new home, however. The Tomlins had given them some bedding, cooking utensils and other odds and ends to start housekeeping. Tess appreciated their kindness, but her heart sank whenever she thought of all the things they still needed.

The second day after the move, a middle–aged woman came to the house, bearing a cardboard box filled with dishes.

"My mother has moved in with me, so we won't be needing this extra set of dishes," she smiled. "They're still in good condition. I thought maybe you could use them."

Tess accepted the offering with a mumbled thanks. "But I don't understand," she said. "How did you find out about us—about what happened?"

"I read about it in the morning newspaper."

Tess found the item on the third page and read it after the woman had left. It was a human–interest story describing their plight, and it included their new address. Plainly, the information had been given to the newspaper by the Tomlins, wanting to bring public attention to a worthy need.

The woman was the first of many who came during the next few days, all of them bringing something—bed linens, towels, lamps. One man came with his son, and the boy gave Jerry some of his toys.

They were all kind, warmhearted people, giving out of true generosity, all of them residents of the city Tess had thought so cold and unfeeling. She found she could no longer hang onto the bitterness that had been with her for the past two months.

There were good people everywhere, she realized, not only in this city, but in every corner of the world. They came forth when they were needed to minister to the sick and crippled, the lonely shut–ins, to offer a helping hand to victims of misfortune like her family.

"It's been like a miracle, hasn't it, Tess?" Steve said. "So many people have been so kind and generous with what they have to give. It's had the effect, I'd say, of giving us a whole new lease on life."

"Yes, Steve, I know what you mean," Tess answered softly. "It seems that God is still working miracles in today's world. We have a lot to be thankful for."

Standing at the window, she gazed at the small, brownstone church in the next block. It must be very convenient for the people who live in the neighborhood, she thought, to have a church so close. She wondered what time they held services on Sunday morning, and whether that was the church the Tomlins attended.

Tess would have to find out.

Agnes Kempton

Goodbye, Mr. Parker

Sally sank deeper into her chair as she gazed out the window. The fog had lifted slightly, and things were becoming visible again. She didn't know whether she was glad or not.

"Here," her husband Dave said, handing her a cup of coffee. He set it on the end table and then sat down opposite her to begin reading the morning paper. Sally said nothing but began sipping the coffee.

Finally Dave wadded up the paper and put it aside. "Come on, Sally. You've been to funerals before. Fred Parker was ready to die. It was what he wanted, wasn't it?"

Her blue eyes clouded and she swallowed hard. "Yes," she said in a hoarse whisper. "He wanted to be with his wife." She turned to face her husband. "He was such a wonderful man."

Walking over to the patio doors, she looked across the lot to the small white house surrounded by shrubbery. Sally hadn't met Mr. Parker until one morning about a month after his wife had died. He knocked at their door and introduced himself. Sally's memory flashed across her mind, recalling the conversation as if it were yesterday.

"My name is Fred Parker," he had said. "I live in the white house across the way and I wonder if you would know anyone who would come in and clean my house once a week."

What was it about this man? Sally had wondered. He was rather tall with thin gray hair and pale blue eyes and a marked gentleness in his voice.

"My wife passed away five weeks ago," he said quietly. "I could have run an ad in the paper, but I thought possibly you might know of someone who would do that type of work."

"Well," she said reluctantly, "I don't really."

He nodded. "Thanks, anyway. I'm sorry I interrupted your day."

"Oh, not at all," she said quickly. As he turned to leave, she called after him. "Mr. Parker, I don't know any cleaning ladies, but if you're not too fussy—well, I'd be glad to do it."

He looked at her a moment, then smiled. "That would be just fine."

After he left she wondered what had possessed her to volunteer, but as time passed she never regretted it. Now her memory was full of those Wednesday mornings spent at Mr. Parker's. She reflected on the morning he told her he was getting an organ.

"I love listening to the organ," Sally said.

"It will fill some vacant hours. I'm so lonesome," he had said, breaking down and silently weeping.

Sally remembered how her heart had gone out to him. After that, she began taking her daughter Erin along on cleaning days. Erin and Mr. Parker had clicked immediately—Erin with the simplicity of a three-year-old and Mr. Parker with the gentleness of age. He would sit Erin on the organ bench beside him and tell her, to her delight, that she could push the keys. From the first day Sally brought Erin, he had put out a dish of butterscotch candies. Each week they were put there for Erin to enjoy.

At one point, Dave had asked his wife why she had kept Mr. Parker's cleaning job for so long. Sally remembered having trouble putting it into words. There was something about being around Fred Parker that was just inspiring. She had never met anyone like him.

She glanced down at the paper where Dave had tossed it on the floor. Even that reminded her of Mr. Parker. He would drive to the newsstand daily to get the paper. And when he read something funny he would sit and chuckle. What a heavenly sense of humor he had. Now, she thought a little bitterly, there would only be about three lines in the paper to close his existence: "Fred J. Parker, born 1894, died 1974. No survivors. Services will be held at the Community Church at ten o'clock Wednesday."

Another Wednesday stood out in her mind. She had been cleaning the kitchen when Mr. Parker had walked in.

"I was writing out instructions for my burial," he had said, pouring himself a glass of orange juice.

"Well, I hope you won't be needing them for a long time," Sally had replied.

He had stood silently a few moments and then finally spoke. "I've often times wondered why the good Lord leaves me here."

"You've done a lot of nice things for a lot of people, Mr. Parker."

"Oh, I keep busy," he had said. "I still enjoy my photography." That was evident from the pictures all through the house—beautiful photographs taken by a professional. "I take naps and go to the store and post office, but I don't feel like I'm really doing anything useful. So why am I here?"

"I think that God leaves you here for people like me," Sally had told him. "People who see your honesty and character. It gives us strength and a hope that we can be more like that. People respect you, Mr. Parker, and the world is a better place because of you."

He had placed his glass on the counter and said, half–smiling and half–crying, "You're putting me on."

"No, I mean it," Sally had insisted.

He then had walked to the foot of the stairs and turned around, smiling. "I think you'd better write that down for me."

Sally turned to Dave. "I'm going to do it," she said firmly.

"Going to do what?"

"I'm going to put it in writing, just as he had asked. I'm going to write an article about Mr. Parker for the paper. He was not simply born and then died. He lived and loved and was one of the kindest human beings I've ever met."

Dave kissed his wife gently on the forehead and wrapped his arms around her. "You're not bad yourself," he said softly.

A few minutes later, Sally sat at her typewriter and closed her eyes tightly. "Dear God," she prayed, "please help me write a tribute worthy of Fred Parker."

Just then she felt a hand on her shoulder. She smiled up at Dave.

"Feeling better?" he asked.

"Yes," she replied.

Sally looked across the lot to the small house. As she did, the sun poked through the fog and the room began to brighten.

"Goodbye, Mr. Parker," she whispered in her heart. As her fingers moved over the keys she smiled and felt renewed—and that was the way Fred Parker would have wanted it.

Charlene Hoyt

Bone in the Soup

Mathilda woke that morning to the smell of fresh-baked bread. In the kitchen, Hedwig von Haartman, captain of The Salvation Army in Finland, was baking *rieska,* a flat bread made of potato and barley flours. Mathilda heard the scrape of the long, wooden spatula as her friend pulled the bread out of the oven.

From her narrow window, Mathilda saw a typical Finnish early morning, with blackness like the inside of a cooking kettle. She heard wind that tromboned down the narrow street in Helsingfors where she rented a room from The Salvation Army. The hail rattled against the glass like steel springs.

"Come on, legs, bend," Mathilda coaxed. "That's it, now joints, all together, and we'll make it upright!" She winced from the pain in her broken ankle that had never healed properly because she had gone off on a train to say goodbye to prisoners headed for Siberia, instead of to a doctor.

She always wore black, with a silver brooch at her neck. The words *Armo ja Rauha* (grace and peace) were carved on it. *Hopefully,* Mathilda mused, *the prisoners will be led to think of God first, before they notice I am only a woman.*

"Good morning, Baroness," Hedwig greeted her. It was their little joke. She was a tall, ruddy–cheeked woman who smiled widely.

"Don't 'baroness' me, captain," Mathilda retorted with good nature. "That life ended when Father died. Everyone at Fakola jail calls me the prisoner's friend, and so I am. Today, I must speak to Matti again."

"The man who tried to steal your brooch?"

Mathilda sipped hot coffee and bit hungrily into the *rieska*. "He never meant to steal it. He asked to hold it in his hands for an hour. Then he returned it, looking so pleased with himself. I don't understand him. He is a life–termer and will die in prison. He has heard the gospel so many times, but I long to know if he has accepted Christ as Savior. He has been so quiet lately."

"Sullen?"

"Not sullen. Quiet. Depressed, or perhaps making escape plans. Who knows a prisoner's heart? Only the Lord who loves him. We are all prisoners until Christ sets us free."

Hedwig offered Mathilda a small dish. "Look, a bit of marmalade!"

Mathilda's hand twitched to accept it, but she shook her head. She ate only prisoner's fare, and the prisoners knew it. "Thank you, no,"

"The Salvation Army meetings are going well," Hedwig said. "We rented a circus tent. People are starved to hear the word of God."

"And you can speak it to them in all the many languages you know," Mathilda replied. Hedwig had been a teacher before joining The Salvation Army.

"Here's some leftover rice pudding," Hedwig insisted. "You must take it to keep your strength up."

Mathilda knew a sensible argument when she heard one. She took a few spoonfuls of the scrumptious treat.

"Wrap up good," said Hedwig. "Take the extra scarf. And hurry home for supper, Tilda, I made *hernekeitto* (pea soup)!" Mathilda turned the possibility over in her mind as she braced against the wind. Pea soup at day's end, a delightful prospect. Lately, her stomach pains came and went at the oddest times. She felt so weak, but she didn't dare miss a day of visiting the prisoners.

Some of the men were in irons, chained to the wall of their cells. They looked forward to seeing a visitor. There was a chaplain who did his duty, but nobody loved the prisoners or thought they could be—or deserved to be—reformed. Mathilda usually spent fifteen minutes in each cell, speaking quietly and patiently, not preaching, but talking of God's great love for them.

Once a murderer had tried to wring her neck, but she had looked him steadily in the eyes and said, "God will not allow this." He had backed away, amazed at her courage.

Most of the time, she listened. "In chapel, they get talked to," she had explained to Hedwig, "but nobody ever listens to them." She often heard tales of crime and depravity that terrified her soul.

"Good morning." She greeted the warden, who only scowled. Like everyone else, he did not approve of a former baroness visiting men who lived like animals.

Matti, the prisoner Mathilda had been anxious to visit, sat on the floor of his damp, cold cell. The body irons had been left off for a few days. He had a long, thin face, folded into itself and creased from loss of body fat, but today he was smiling.

In his filthy outstretched hand she saw a delicate ivory brooch with the words *Armo ja Rauha* carved in the center. "Beautiful!" she cried. "The exact image of my silver brooch, but much lovelier. Did you make it? Where did you get ivory?"

"For you, Miss Wrede," he said, his eyes shining. "Will you wear it? Seven months ago I had a really bad bowl of cabbage soup one night for supper. Not a bit of meat, not even a vegetable peeling. Just greasy water with a big piece of bone. I saved the bone and washed it and dried it for weeks in the sun every day. Then I worked on the carving with a little nail I found."

"I remember you borrowed my silver pin for an hour," Mathilda interrupted.

"Yes, to fix the design in my mind. For months I carved it, wanting to give you a gift for your sacrifice in coming here to visit us."

Mathilda's eyes teared. "Lovely," she said again. She held it in her hand and wondered over the seven months of painstaking work that fashioned it.

"Miss Wrede, that is not all!" Matti hunched forward in his eagerness. "Out of a soup bone, I have made something beautiful, yes. But I am the bone in the soup, Miss! I, Matti, as bad as any man ever born, was finally made into something good by God. This bone was probably from a cow that died of old age. I'm like the cow, and soon to die for my crimes. I remember how many times you told me that the God of love could save a man like me and turn him into something fine. His Son has cleaned up my sins, like the sun bleached the bone white.

"Soon I will die for my crimes. I die a sinner, but a pardoned sinner. Me, Matti, just a bone in the soup, for His crown."

Mathilda was speechless. She could not add anything to his testimony of joy, so she listened. She listened while hours passed and she knew streets would be dark and deserted and Hedwig would be heating up the pea soup.

As Matti began his life story for the umpteenth time, Mathilda thought of the first prisoners she had ever seen in Vasa, where her father was governor and she lived in a big house with a maid to wait on her and a beautiful room to herself. Her pretty carved furniture had been made by prisoners, but that meant nothing to her until she had seen them one day in the street, chained together, beaten and driven like oxen.

She had been converted to Christ at age eight and wondered what to do with her life. That day in the street, God seemed to call her to help the prisoners. "I am too young, just a girl," she objected.

At home, she had opened her Bible for guidance. "Say not, I am a child: for thou shalt go to all that I shall send thee, and whatsoever I command thee thou shalt speak" (Jer. 1:6–7 KJV).

Startled, she let the Bible fall open to Ezekiel. Staring up at her were the words: "Go, get thee to them of the captivity" (Ezek. 3:11).

Now she was here, years later, still being a friend to prisoners. God kept opening doors and blessing her work. She realized Matti was bidding her "good night," so she rose.

She heard cries from all the other cells. "Miss Wrede! We have waited all day to see you! Some of us have not talked to you for weeks! Don't go yet. Please don't go!"

Mathilda nodded patiently. "I will stay a while longer. You may come one at a time to the vacant cell where the warden has given me a little table and chair."

For just a moment she imagined candles twinkling in every window on the streets, late workers hurrying home to warm houses and hot food, the friendly sign over the Salvation Army building . . . and Hedwig warming up the pea soup with leftover *rieska*.

Then she settled herself on the chair and opened her Bible. Removing the silver pin at her throat, she dropped it into her dress pocket. That belonged to her old life as baroness. She fastened the pin of bone at her neck. She would always wear it.

Lois Hoadley Dick

Chance Encounter

She stood in the open doorway of her apartment house. She could feel the cold, brisk air on her face as it attempted to push through her into the warm security of the apartment building. She could feel the warm air from the hallway pressing against the nape of her neck, almost as a plea for her to close the door.

Anna Marie Koller was filled with doubts and fear as she faced the steps of her small apartment building which led to the New York street. She knew she was being pushed by a hidden force to make this journey, but she was terrified of the outcome. For two days she had harbored her secret, and she was now at the bursting point. She must go and talk to the man, even though she knew it would probably end in death—hers or his.

Her mind made up, Anna Marie stepped onto the porch, closing the door firmly. She decided she would never enter that door again until her mission was complete. Slowly she walked down the stairway, turned right on the sidewalk, and headed for the subway entrance a block away. As she walked, she thought about the terrible things that had happened so long ago, yet they were so vivid in her memory.

Her family had thought they were safe, but the Gestapo had found them hiding in the barn of one her father's employees. They had been living in the barn for almost four years, and the summer of 1944 should have been a time of rejoicing. The Allies had landed in France, and the end of the war was rumored to be close. Instead, they had been taken to a railroad station, herded into an open cattle car, and with a few hundred more people transported across Holland into Germany. They had arrived in a little town that was on the outskirts of a large concentration camp.

As they were forced off the train, they underwent an inspection by the military guards. Anna Marie's fifteen–year–old sister was forcefully removed from her mother's arms to stand with other young girls. Her mother begged for her sister to be returned to the family, but the guard's only answer was to slap her in the mouth, cutting her lip. Anna Marie's father took a handkerchief out of his pocket and very gently dabbed the blood from his wife's mouth. Anna Marie never again saw her sister.

The others were shoved into a barracks–like room, where they all slept together. For two months they lived in these rooms—ill–fed, without heat or medical attention and with the crudest of sanitary facilities.

One fall day they were all herded into the compound and told they would be leaving their camp, marching to another installation forty–two miles away. Anyone who attempted to escape would be immediately shot. Anyone who fell and did not get up to complete the march would be shot. It was expected, they were told, that all prisoners would reach the camp. The gates were flung open and they were pushed out into the harsh roadway to make their long journey.

Anna Marie vividly remembered her mother stumbling, falling to the ground and saying she could walk no more. The guard, a young SS corporal named Rudi Weber, demanded that she pick herself up and continue marching. Anna Marie remembered the complete look of exhaustion on her mother's face as the corporal pointed his rifle at her and shouted for her to march. Anna Marie remembered her mother fainting, the shot of the rifle, and the reaction of rage in her father as he rushed at the guard. Anna Marie remembered the guard pointing his rifle at her father and firing. Anna Marie was seven years old when it happened.

Today—thirty–four years later—Anna Marie still vividly remembered it all—and she remembered the face of Rudi Weber. She had seen that same face two days before in a New York subway and had followed the man to an apartment in upper Manhattan. She had gone back the next morning to await his departure and had followed him to his place of employment. And for one full day she sat in her apartment, ignoring her husband and her children, contemplating revenge. Anna Marie was on her way to kill Rudi Weber.

As she rode the subway toward Weber's residence, she thought about her life since that terrible day when she lost her family. She thought about the kind Dutch family that had adopted her. She thought about the American GI that she had met and married when she was twenty–two years old. She thought about her life in New York, how her children had grown to become outstanding students at high school and college. She thought about her conversion to Christianity, and how her faith in God had given her and her family the strength to face life with more confidence than they had ever felt before. She thought about her pastor and felt a twinge of guilt at the knowledge that he might find out what she was doing. She thought about her husband and how, even though she had never kept a secret from him before, she had not told him of her encounter with Rudi Weber.

But her most pressing thought was revenge for her mother and father's death.

The subway stopped. She slowly walked toward the open door and pressed with the crowd toward the escalator that took her to the street level. Turning left, she walked three blocks to the apartment house that she had seen Rudi Weber enter. Looking at the nameplates, she could not determine which apartment was his. There was no Weber listed. This was something she had not anticipated. Walking back into the street, she glanced at the twenty–five stories of the apartment house. She would never find him in that huge building, she thought. Then she realized that a former Nazi living in hiding would surely not use his own name.

She had hoped to be in his apartment when he arrived from work, but that now seemed impossible. Walking across the street, she stopped and waited for him to appear from the subway. When she saw him walking down the street, she confidently crossed the street and walked in behind him. As he turned into the apartment doorway, she followed. As he put the key into the lock and opened the door, she waited for him to walk through and then smiled and said, "Thank you." As he walked toward the elevator, she followed. When he entered, she also entered. When the elevator stopped at his floor and he stepped out, she also stepped out. When he turned left and headed towards the door of his apartment, she followed. When he stopped in front of the door and glanced at her in a questioning way, she stopped.

"Can I help you?" he asked.

"Yes, you can, Corporal Rudi Weber," she said.

His smile evaporated. She thought she saw a hint of fear in his eyes. "You must be mistaken. You must have me confused with someone else."

"No, Herr Weber, I do not have you mistaken with anyone. I know who you are. I recognized you immediately when I saw you two days ago. I know you don't remember me, but you murdered my mother and father. Now I have come to avenge their deaths."

Slowly, her hand came out of her coat pocket. She was holding her husband's small caliber revolver.

Looking first at the revolver then back into the determined face of Anna Marie, Rudi Weber resigned himself to the inevitable. "Yes, I am Rudi Weber. I have lived all these years with the fear that I would be found out. But I hope you will believe me when I say that I am really sorry for what I did in my youth. I was a young man then, following orders—"

"That's what all you Nazis said!" screamed Anna Marie, her nerves taut with the pressure of the moment. "They all said that they were only following orders. I too am following orders right now! I am following a higher order by killing you. 'An eye for an eye and a tooth for a tooth.'"

"Yes, being a Jew, you would quote that Old Testament saying. But you see, I am now a Christian. I am fully committed to a new life in Jesus Christ. In fact, I now volunteer all my extra time down at the New Life Mission in the Bowery in an attempt to atone for my past deeds." Words gushed from his mouth, rushing to finish before his certain death. "I know that my sins are forgiven, but I still feel guilty.

Please, before you kill me, at least let me tell you about the new life that I have found in Jesus Christ."

The words came at Anna Marie like a bolt of lightning. *What would the pastor say,* she thought, *if he knew I was planning to kill someone?*

"Jesus forgave His tormentors and murderers," she could hear him say. "So you should forgive those who have tormented and murdered your loved ones." The pastor's voice was so vivid in her mind that she quickly turned to see where he might be standing. But he was not there. She turned back to Rudi.

He stood there, tears running down his cheeks.

"Please," he said, "forgive me. Kill me if you will, but forgive me for hurting you so deeply."

Anna Marie looked at Rudi Weber. The heavy weight on her shoulders was pressing her into the floor. She felt confused. She did not know what to do. Should she forgive him, or kill him? Both of these solutions were in her power.

She looked into the frightened but somehow peaceful eyes of her captive. Then she realized with a shock that within the last two days all her peace in Christ had disappeared, overwhelmed by her consuming desire for revenge. Along with the desire for revenge had come a heavy, aching burden on her heart. Would it ever go away? Would her peace ever return?

These thoughts flashed through her mind as she stared into the eyes of Rudi Weber. What to do, what to do? Slowly she lowered her hand and put the gun back into her coat pocket.

"Yes," she said, but no more words would come out. The lump in her throat was choking her. Tears welled in her eyes, but she felt the power, presence and peace of God very close to her. She slowly turned and started walking toward the elevator. The burden on her shoulders was lifted. The years of bitterness for her family's death were wiped away with her one word of forgiveness.

Captain Russell Fritz

Silenced Gods

The old man's eyes were wide open even before the sun had begun to saturate the dark corners of the room. He was thinking of the voices. He frowned and swallowed hard and thought how unusual it was. His ancestors had been speaking to him for the past forty years, and now suddenly they were fading away. In their place, there was a confusion of voices, of strange noises.

"I must have incurred their wrath," he thought, and was afraid.

Lying still on the bed, he stared at the wooden cupboard standing against the wall. He had been told that he was born under the auspicious moon of the snake god, who had paid him a visit on the night of his birth. They said his spirit had a close connection to the realm of the gods and goddesses so that he could hear them. They told him he could hear his departed ancestors speak in a way few men could.

He wasn't sure anymore. Lately he had been groping, searching. He had to think, to be reminded, to reassure himself.

The lower edges of the sky were beginning to lighten, and the old man blinked. His wife stirred in bed. They got up silently and moved to the kitchen. The old woman removed a metal pot hanging from a peg on the low ceiling and began to cook porridge. The old man's youngest son entered the room. He was a tall young man. There was an awkward air about him, as if being in his father's presence made him uncomfortable. He put down his bag.

"Good morning, Pa," he greeted his father.

The old man did not look up from his meal, but acknowledged his son's presence with a gruff "Umm."

His son was studying electrical engineering at the National University in the city. Engineering, science . . . these were things the older man knew little about. What he knew, the world he lived in and the air he breathed, whispered of luck, of ancestors to be appeased, of spirits and gods and of inauspicious moons to be avoided.

The man took a bus to work every morning. As it pulled up to the bus stop, he looked out to see the large hand that was painted on the sign outside his shop. The palm was open and outstretched, as if it were catching in its painted fingers the rays of sun that were sliding over the gleaming sign. It was the palm of fortune.

The old man had two customers that morning—both middle–aged women. The first wanted to find a date for her next *mah–jongg* game she would be holding for the other women in the neighborhood. The second wanted to know if she could keep the man she was married to under her roof.

He perused the second woman's palm. He searched it and read the lines, the creases, the bumps. Then he sat back, his eyes closed in intense concentration. He was departing from this world, slipping into that realm of voices—that safe, comfortable realm he had known for so long and never questioned.

There was bad news for this lady. Her luck lines were crossed. She would lose her husband to another woman. Perhaps. Perhaps not. The blood seemed to rush to his head, keeping out the voices that told him what he should say to her.

He could hear the voices now and again, but they were faint and drawing silent. Another sound was taking them away. It was too loud. It was drowning them out.

He looked at the face of the woman. She was staring at him the way they all did—with trust. He nodded and started writing on a piece of paper. His fingers were cold.

The old man took off that afternoon to go to the nearby temple. He spoke to the temple priests and told them his problem. The priests burnt some prayer paper to the snake god, then they asked the old man to drink the ashes in a cup of tepid water. They said that would be sufficient to break the curse that was cutting off this fortune–teller from the voices of his ancestors.

As the old man sat in the bus on his way home, he wondered what kind of power could be so great as to break the communication that had existed so long between him and his ancestors.

Chinese New Year came the next week. The day after the holiday, his youngest son brought his girlfriend from the university home with him for the first time. She was timid and shy and smiled politely as she entered the little village home.

The son brought her toward the old man. "This is my father."

The young woman noticed that the old man was staring at the cross hanging from a simple gold chain around her neck. The son had made it for her as a gift when he found out she was a Christian. She had worn it around her neck ever since. He had requested her not to wear the cross to his house on that day. "My father will not understand," he had said. She argued and said that she would hide the cross under her blouse. On the way over, it had slipped out and now lay displayed simply and prominently around her throat.

"You are Chinese, but you are Christian?" the old man asked. His voice, as always, was hard. But his eyes were kind, and the young woman drew courage from this.

"Yes, I am Chinese. And I am also Christian."

The son stood beside his girlfriend. His hand tightened around her waist.

The old man frowned, but then he nodded and asked the girl to come and wish his wife and the rest of the family a happy Chinese New Year. The young couple relaxed.

It was getting late when the son left the group in the living room. He was looking for his father. He walked to the back of the house and saw his father standing in the backyard with his hands clasped behind his back. The old man heard his son approaching.

The father did not look directly at his son as he spoke. He simply said, "She is a good girl."

The son smiled in the shadows. He was relieved. He waited.

Crickets rubbed their wings. A frog burped in a steady beat, "arrp . . . arrp . . . arrp . . . "

The father's voice was soft, almost reluctant. He said, "Tell her to stop praying for us."

The son wanted to say something, but stopped. Instead he nodded his head and turned around to go back into the house. The old man continued standing by himself and staring into the confusing lines of the dark sky. His lips started moving rapidly as he looked on the moon. Then he thought, perhaps one day he would get that young lady to tell him about this God of hers. This God that was so powerful.

Perhaps one day.

The crickets rubbed on.

Maeli Wong

A Gift of Snow

Just inside the big picture window Emma sat in her rocking chair watching the snowflakes float gently to the ground. They were white and clean against the sleeping earth, but those that fell on the sidewalk and street disappeared as if never having existed. The early darkness of winter shut out the unlit room behind her, but through her window she could see the streetlights flicker on.

Back and forth rocked the chair, carrying her slight body in its soothing arc. The children, where were the children? They always appeared with the first snow. She stopped her rocking, hoping to hear their shouts of joy at discovering the coming of heaven's ice cream, a delicacy to catch on tongues.

She listened. No children. Only the swish and slush of turning wheels on the street. It was too dark now. There would be no children tonight.

Emma began to rock again, allowing the movement to carry her into tomorrow. Tomorrow the snow would cover the brown, and the children would build her a snowman with a stick nose and stone eyes. She would call to them from her doorway and offer them warm cookies from the oven. They would smile up at her.

A voice called out her name. She rocked harder. No! She would stay here. She would not leave. The children still might come.

"Mrs. Taylor," the voice insisted. "You'll miss your dinner." A light came on in the room and chased the darkness away.

Emma sighed. The light always brought her back. Nurse Pickens came and laid a professionally gentle hand on the thin shoulder. Emma let her help her up out of the chair and guide her down the short hallway, through the smell of antiseptic, into the dining room of the Claremont Home for the Aged.

It wasn't a bad dining room with its cool green walls and white starched tablecloths. Usually Emma looked forward to mealtime. It was a time to gather and socialize. Most of the time the conversation centered around the weather, the nurses, the visitors and memories. Yes, most of all, old memories. Tonight Emma wanted only to sit alone and dream through the falling flakes outside her window. It was Christmas Eve.

Many of the seats were empty. Clara, George and Louise were missing. They had gone to spend the holidays with relatives. At least they had some place to go, had someone to take them. They would have moments to hang onto for one more year.

Henry shared the table in the corner with her. Emma was thankful, for Henry rarely talked. *I'm ninety–two years old,* she thought. *What's left to talk about?*

After dinner Emma crossed the hall to the sitting room with the others. It was a comfortable room, furnished from another period of life, and she had always liked it. It reminded her of days when she was younger. A Christmas tree in one corner proclaimed the season with twinkling lights that reflected against the gleaming glass ornaments.

Emma took the side of the sofa closest to the tree. She should be happy. Here it was—the eve of the greatest celebration on earth. She should be rejoicing, but she couldn't stop the feeling of sadness, the loneliness, the terrible loneliness.

Nurse Pickens came in pushing a tray piled high with cookies, paper plates, cups, coffee and tea.

"Mrs. Taylor," she said offering Emma the first choice from the cookie plate. "Are you all right?"

It was the first time Emma had seen the nurse in street clothes. Without the white uniform Nurse Pickens' entire personality seemed to warm. Her hair, usually pulled into a tight little bun at the nape of her neck, was allowed to fall freely about her shoulders. She appeared much younger now.

"I'm fine," Emma said. She chose two pink frosted pinwheels from the tray. "I'm just tired, I guess." Nurse Pickens smiled and moved on.

Yes, thought Emma, *I am tired.* She looked down at the Nativity scene beneath the pine. The baby Jesus seemed to be looking right back at her. A frail Virgin Mary knelt beside her Babe with a loving hand laid upon His head.

How Emma wished that she had had a child. A daughter would have been nice. One who would have invited her to her home on nights like this. One who would have given her grandchildren to love, to fondle, to spoil.

After her marriage she had waited, hoping to discover that she carried a life within herself. Months passed, then years, and finally she had given up all hope. It hadn't been bad, just the two them, but now John was gone. How long now? Twenty years? No, it couldn't be. Had she really been alone that long?

She looked down again at the Babe. Such a long time. She wished the loneliness would end. Why couldn't it be over? What was left? Nothing. *Dear Jesus, let it be over,* she prayed.

"Mrs. Taylor?"

Emma came back to the scene around her. A young girl stood smiling at her.

"My name is Judy Anderson. Can I get you anything?"

Emma hesitated a moment. She was about to say no, but instead she said, "Yes, please, could I have a cup of tea? Just a little sugar."

Emma watched as the girl prepared the tea at the serving cart. She had not seen her come in and Emma thought she could not be more than fifteen years old—her whole life ahead of her.

The tea was hot and soothing, and Emma sipped it appreciatively.

"Is it very cold outside?" Emma asked Judy, who sat next to her on the couch.

"Oh, yes," the girl answered. "I had to run to keep warm."

Emma laughed. "I wish I could still run." She was immediately sorry she had said it. It made the girl uneasy and at a loss for words.

Emma noticed the smooth complexion and the alert brown eyes. She was a lovely child. Emma liked her, but she realized the tremendous gap between them, more than three–quarters of a century.

"Judy, why are you here?"

The girl appeared puzzled at the question.

"I mean," Emma continued, "it's Christmas Eve. Surely you would prefer to be with your family."

Judy smiled shyly. She reached over and touched Emma's wrinkled hand. "I see my family every day. This year I felt as if I wanted to do something special for someone at Christmas."

Judy looked away from the gaze of the old woman. Others around the room were engaged in conversation. Only Emma sat alone. At first it had been this segregation that had made Judy approach her. Now it was something else. It was Emma's appearance. The dark patterned dress, the bib apron, the white hair gathered in a twisted circle at the back of the neck—all fit Judy's image of what an old–fashioned grandmother should look like. Judy had seen only faded pictures of her own grandmother.

They sat for a long time in silence. Emma wondered what life was like now for a young girl growing up. Oh, she read the papers now and then, watched a little television. It was a turbulent world. How did one talk to a youngster of today?

Judy stole sidewise glances at Emma. What did one say to a senior citizen? Coming here to the home for the aged had seemed like a good idea. But now what?

Someone began to sing. One by one the others joined in the carol. The voices wavered over the high notes and occasionally someone forgot the words, but they forged on. Someone dimmed the lights as they drifted into a shaky rendition of "Silent Night." The brilliance of the Christmas tree now became the object of everyone's attention.

Emma leaned over and whispered to Judy, "Do you think it's still snowing?"

Judy whispered back, "Why don't we go and see?"

Quietly they rose and left the gathering. Judy proffered a helping arm, and they crossed into the darkened dining room. Judy opened the curtains. The snow was falling heavily now.

"I love the snow," said Emma. "The children of the neighborhood always built me a snowman." She sighed.

Judy pulled a chair from the nearest table and offered it to Emma. The old woman stared out at the snow and described the childhood winters she had spent on her parents' farm in Minnesota. She talked of skiing to school on homemade skis, of horse drawn sleighs, and of the fear of losing one's way in the blinding blizzards.

Judy was entranced. She had never heard anyone talk of life like this. It was life as it was fifty, sixty, even seventy years ago.

Emma talked until she realized that the activity in the next room had stopped and Nurse Pickens had appeared in the doorway.

"Mrs. Taylor? Is that you?"

Judy answered her. "I'm sorry. I didn't realize it was so late."

"It's all right, Judy, but I think that Mrs. Taylor should be getting some rest now."

She handed Judy a brown furry coat and a crazily striped stocking cap that dangled almost to the floor when she placed it on her head. Emma thought it was the ugliest hat she had ever seen.

That night, Emma left the window curtains open. She fell asleep thinking about Judy and watching the snow.

The next morning she woke early. There were no sounds yet. The snow had stopped. She turned onto her back to relieve the ache in it. She thought again of Judy. The girl had promised to come again soon to see her. *She won't come,* Emma thought. *Why would a young girl like that waste her time with an old woman like me?* She was certain she would never see her again.

Emma got up slowly and with some difficulty managed to wiggle into her robe. She had decided to sit by the window and admire the snow before the cars turned it into gray slush. As she lowered herself into the rocking chair she stared at the scene that met her eyes.

There, not ten feet away, was the biggest snowman she had ever seen! Two stones for eyes looked back at her, and a ridiculously crooked stick projected a nose.

On its head, precariously dangling almost to the ground, was a crazy striped stocking cap of outrageous color.

Emma thought it was the most beautiful hat she had ever seen.

Linette L. Wheeler

Facing the Inevitable

"Well, here you are," Charles Foster told himself as he stepped into the room he had always occupied during his visits home. "Home for Christmas."

Christmas? There was little pleasure in the thought. The iron bed, the highboy, the high school mementos—nothing had changed, yet everything was different.

Charles undressed quickly. Later, lying in bed, he pondered the events of the day. For weeks he had fortified himself against the inevitable question, "How is it, son, with your soul?"

But there had been none of that. And there wouldn't be. He should be relieved. But he wasn't. His father's illness left him cold.

"How is Dad?" he had asked his mother when he arrived.

"Weak, of course," she had responded. "The last attack was hard on him."

"And his mind?" Charles hated the question. That there should be any question about the mental capacities of a man as well–educated and dedicated as his evangelist father was inconceivable.

His mother hesitated. She has aged, Charles told himself, as he noted the stark whiteness of her hair and the tiny lines of worry when she smiled.

"There's one thing we can be grateful for," she said. "His personality hasn't changed. Though he is seldom rational, he is always happy."

"I'm glad," Charles said, his mind suddenly overwhelmed by memories of a fun–filled youth.

"But I have to admit it isn't easy," his mother continued. "Knowing how much he feared becoming useless . . ." She stopped. A faraway look crept into her eyes.

He should have come home sooner. Charles knew that now. But he hadn't known that things were this bad. He had been told about the heart attacks. At first his father wrote that he would cut down on his evangelistic meetings. Later, that he had decided to retire. "I'm not much good anymore." Those were his words.

"You'll never be useless, Dad," Charles answered.

But it wasn't until recently that he had been informed his father was failing mentally.

"You're in for a shock," his mother had told him when Charles wrote that he would be spending Christmas with them. "It's very possible he won't know you."

"Why doesn't the doctor do something?" Charles had asked.

"The arteries to the brain are affected."

"Isn't there any cure?"

"Not for people as severely affected as he. Tranquilizers help when he is restless. But he needs constant watching. A neighbor comes in part of the day." His mother reached over and touched his arm. "I'm glad you're home. I need you, Charles. But, come, let's go to him. I'll tell Mrs. Simpson she can leave."

Mother and son entered the room together. Seeing Charles, Mr. Foster smiled broadly as he stretched out his frail hands to greet him.

"Charles!" he cried. "Why didn't you tell me you were coming?"

His father did know him!

"Dad, it's so good to see you." Charles led his father to a nearby rocker. "Here, sit down and tell me all about yourself."

"You've grown," his father said as he settled his tall frame in a padded rocking chair. "Must be six feet now, aren't you? Prosperous, too, I see." He grinned mischievously as he thumbed the rich tweed of his son's suit. "Seeing you makes me think of the time we hunted wild horses in Taylor's Canyon. Remember those days?"

Charles raised questioning eyebrows. He had never hunted wild horses!

"Let it be. Just agree with him," his mother softly cautioned. "It's better that way."

Later she explained, "His doctor believes that in moments of excitement, increased heart action forces blood through the arteries to the brain. Often clear, logical thinking results—as it did when your father greeted you. But did you notice how quickly he became confused? He thought you were his brother. When this happens, we just play along with him. We are whoever he says we are." She bit her lip, her eyes misty.

"He doesn't always sleep the whole night through. Often when he's awake for any length of time he relives some phase of his life as a clergyman. Some nights he conducts business meetings. At other times he performs wedding ceremonies. When he asks a question I respond." She stopped. Charles realized her emotions were getting the best of her. But she went on.

"When Mary and Jim were home, even the children played our little game. One night when he called for a vote on a motion, tiny Jean answered, 'Aye' with the rest of us." Now her voice broke. Charles put his arm around her shoulder and drew her close.

"Oh, Charles, it's almost more than I can bear. I'm so ashamed of myself. But time after time I find myself crying, 'Why, Lord? Why?'"

Charles swallowed with difficulty. There was nothing he could say. The injustice of the situation overwhelmed him. He simply stroked his mother's thinning hair.

Lying in bed that night, Charles wondered why he wasn't relieved that this year he would escape his father's questions regarding the welfare of his soul. *Escape?* The word's significance frightened him. Now, escape had permanent significance, and there was no joy in the thought.

How far he had drifted, Charles thought. When and where had it begun? First it had been school. The coveted scholarship gave him the excuse he needed to bypass his father's Christian alma mater. Then money and success became important goals in his life. He had studied hard. He had neglected church. But industry had its reward. When he was ready to go to work, he had been offered a position of note. Then clients had to be entertained in the fashion of the day.

Little by little the gap had widened, and he never had bothered to retrace his steps. Now there was no way back. Even his father could not help him. At last he slept.

Charles awoke suddenly. It was dark. Someone was speaking. He raised his head and listened. His father! Just as his mother had said. But this was no business meeting. His father was preaching!

Moving quickly, Charles slipped into his bedroom slippers and robe and hurried to his father's room, but he did not enter. He stopped in the doorway, his tall frame silhouetted in the light that shone through a window in the hall.

"Today is the day of salvation. . . ."

An evangelistic plea? "'For God so loved the world that He gave His only begotten Son that whosoever believeth in Him shall not perish but have everlasting life.'

"Is there anyone here tonight who would like to make Christ the Lord of your life?" He waited. "Yes, I see your hand . . . and yours . . . God bless you . . . and you, by the door?" Charles jumped. His father had seen him! "This is your moment of decision. Will you accept Christ now?"

Charles tried to move, to retreat, but he couldn't. It was as if his slippers were glued to the floor. His pulse quickened. An irresistible power drew him toward the faith he had spurned. He opened his mouth. No, it was too late.

"Will you, my lad, will you?" The words thrust themselves at him.

Then someone moved to his side, and he heard a muffled sob. His mother had joined the pre–dawn evangelistic meeting. He pulled her into his embrace.

"Will you?" Again the question.

Suddenly resistance fled. Charles took a deep breath and, with no pretense, said, "Yes, I will."

"God bless you, my son." His father settled back on his pillow contentedly. In a short time he was asleep.

"And to think your father worried about being useless," his mother whispered as she squeezed her son's arm.

As if in a trance, Charles led his mother back to her room. He tucked her in bed and sat down beside her. Neither spoke for some time. Finally he whispered, "Merry Christmas, Mother."

Christmas? Now there was pleasure in the thought! Their son had truly come home.

Margaret Anderson

The Three Lives of Marie–Louise

When Mathieu heard the clattering of horses' hooves up the street, he went to the door of his bakery and, joining company with a straggle of curious customers, gaped and blinked in the strong sunshine at these strange horsemen, the like of which he had never seen before.

No one in the little group had the slightest idea as to the identity of the cavalrymen, though one old fellow thought they might be Russians. As they trotted by, the sun not only sparkled from their tall lances but glinted from the pistols they levelled at the people on the sidewalks.

At a safe distance, or so he told me twenty years later, Mathieu had followed the horsemen along the *Rue du Marteau* until they came to the *Place du Martyr* and the *Hôtel de Ville*. Two soldiers dismounted and went inside. Within minutes the Belgian flag was pulled down and the standard of Kaiser Wilhelm II's German Empire was displayed in its place. Slowly it dawned on Mathieu that his little town of Verviers, just inside Belgium's eastern frontier, had been invaded—a fact that was confirmed some hours later when a column of dusty, footsore German infantrymen trudged into the town after their long, forced march from Aachen. That day was August 4, 1914.

World War I had begun. The occupation lasted four years.

Also in Verviers at that time of the sudden German invasion was a fourteen–year–old girl named Marie–Louise Debouny who, some six years earlier, had had a rather remarkable religious experience. It should be said that the Debouny family belonged to the minority group of Protestant evangelicals in the town.

When the little girl was eight years old, a strong yearning to talk to God personally had developed—a feeling fostered by the sight of the Christmas tree her father had cut down in nearby Ardennes. The mystery of the great tree enraptured her. She dreamed of climbing to its tip so that, being very high up, she could talk to God alone.

The idea took shape in another way. One day she climbed onto the henhouse, which was close to the Christmas tree. From there, she began to speak to God spontaneously, familiarly. The henhouse had become her place of prayer.

About this time, when out with her mother one day, Marie–Louise overheard a conversation which greatly upset her. René, a neighbor's son, was nearly mute. Marie–Louise decided that she would talk to God personally and ask Him to help the little boy. All alone atop the henhouse, she implored God to heal little René. Suddenly, a delightful idea came to her mind—she could *help* God answer her prayer!

Joining work to faith, she asked permission to take the child out each day. By the bridge, over the tumbling, babbling River Vesdra, which flows through Verviers, Marie–Louise, the eight–year–old, began teaching René how to talk. Day after day she persevered. Slowly, the rebellious tongue was mastered!

Without pride, and in the simplicity of childhood, Marie–Louise rejoiced within herself at this miracle. Henceforth, her faith in God had firm foundations.

Nevertheless, during the German occupation, fear nearly broke her faith into fragments when, by way of reprisals, houses were burned and hostages shot. At this time of sheer terror, the wise pastor of her church reminded her of the story of René—her story—and the nearness of God she had experienced.

"Perfect love casteth out fear," a voice spoke to her that night, and within herself there grew a conviction that she would receive power from God to serve Him, to do all that He asked of her in that place to which He would send her.

By the time Marie–Louise was sixteen, she knew that this service would be overseas. The thought of leaving her family nearly broke her heart, but at a youth camp she received another personal message, "You will become a mother to many who have not one."

After overcoming many obstacles, Marie–Louise arrived in Rwanda as a missionary nurse. For fifteen years she devoted herself to the sick, at times delivering babies in the primitive conditions of the bush. She also managed a school of more than a thousand students. Into those arduous, hazardous years she packed more than a lifetime of experience and compassionate care for others, and her faith never wavered. She truly had become a mother to many who had not one.

Marie–Louise did not return to Verviers until after the end of World War II, thus missing the misery, deprivation and terror of the second occupation. And when she did return, it appeared at first that she had lived out her usefulness, for she came back to her hometown on a stretcher in extreme weakness. Her long period of service in tropical Africa had been exhausting.

Even then, God had some work for her. Greatly restored after a short rest, Marie–Louise was able to assist the local Salvation Army officer who had fallen sick. Later, when the officer had to leave town, it was Marie–Louise who took the leadership of the little group of Salvationists comprising the corps. It seemed inevitably in God's plan that she should become a Salvationist. Thus began her second life.

In 1948, Marie–Louise was called to Brussels to take charge of the infant Goodwill Service of The Salvation Army. For twenty–five years this wonderful little Belgian woman maintained a mammoth program on behalf of the underprivileged in the Belgian capital city until she retired at the age of seventy–three!

Through many years, she helped thousands of people with food parcels, coal, medical care, clothing and sound advice. She visited them in their homes, found work for them, and served them with such competence and ardent thoroughness that the social service and allied governmental departments developed an increasing respect for, and appreciation of, the work of The Salvation Army in Belgium.

Beyond any material aid she could give, Marie–Louise gave comfort and hope in the name of the Savior, to whom she had dedicated herself as a child in the dark days of World War I in occupied Verviers.

What of her third life? During her days in Africa, Marie–Louise adopted an unwanted baby and, in addition to all her other labors for the Kingdom, brought up little Monique as if she were her own child. The girl became a Salvationist and, in due course, an officer and is presently serving with her husband in a position of responsibility. Monique is a testament to the giving spirit of her mother.

Marie–Louise Debouny is an "Envoy Extraordinaire." Never given over to promotion, she would much rather get on with her work than spend time talking about it. Maybe a trifle unorthodox in style but serving the Lord with gladness, with her whole heart and in great humility, Marie–Louise Debouny is remembered with deep gratitude by thousands of Belgian men, women and children in whose hearts she lit candles of hope.

It is a long way back in time to her early "conversations" with God on top of the henhouse, but the three lives of Marie–Louise have proven extraordinarily fruitful, meriting without any doubt a special emphasis when the King eventually says to her, "Inasmuch as ye have done it unto one of the least of these My brethren, ye have done it unto Me."

Lt. Colonel Bernard E. McCarthy

Trouble at the Inn

For years now, whenever Christmas pageants are talked about in a certain little town in the Midwest, someone is sure to mention the name of Wallace Purling. Wally's performance in one annual production of the Nativity play has slipped into the realm of legend. But the old–timers who were in the audience that night never tire of recalling exactly what happened.

Wally was nine that year and in the second grade, though he should have been in the fourth. Most people in town knew that he had difficulty in keeping up. He was big and clumsy, slow in movement and mind. Still, Wally was well liked by the other children in his class, all of whom were smaller than he, though the boys had trouble hiding their irritation when Wally would ask to play ball with them or any game, for that matter, in which winning was important.

Most often they'd find a way to keep him out, but Wally would hang around anyway—not sulking, just hoping. He was always a helpful boy, a willing and smiling one, and the natural protector, paradoxically, of the underdog. Sometimes, if the older boys chased the younger ones away, it would always be Wally who would say, "Can't they stay? They're no bother."

Wally fancied the idea of being a shepherd with a flute in the Christmas pageant that year, but the play's director, Miss Lumbard, assigned him to a more important role. After all, she reasoned, the Innkeeper did not have too many lines, and Wally's size would make his refusal of lodging to Joseph more forceful.

And so it happened that the usual large, partisan audience gathered for the town's yearly extravaganza of crooks and crèches, of beards, crowns, halos and a whole stageful of squeaky voices.

No one on stage or off was more caught up in the magic of the night than Wallace Purling. They said later that he stood in the wings and watched the performance with such fascination that from time to time Miss Lumbard had to make sure he didn't wander onstage before his cue.

The time came when Joseph appeared, guiding Mary to the door of the inn slowly and tenderly. Joseph knocked hard on the wooden door set into the painted backdrop. Wally the Innkeeper was waiting.

"What do you want?" Wally said, swinging the door open with a brusque gesture.

"We seek lodging."

"Seek it elsewhere." Wally looked straight ahead but spoke vigorously. "The inn is filled."

"Sir, we have asked everywhere in vain. We have traveled far and are very weary."

"There is no room in this inn for you." Wally looked properly stern.

"Please, good innkeeper, this is my wife, Mary. She is heavy with child and needs a place to rest. Surely you must have a small corner for her. She is so tired."

Now, for the first time, the Innkeeper relaxed his stiff stance and looked down at Mary. With that, there was a long pause, long enough to make the audience a bit tense with embarrassment.

"No! Begone!" the prompter whispered from the wings.

"No!" Wally repeated automatically. "Begone!"

Joseph sadly placed his arm around Mary. Mary laid her head upon her husband's shoulder and the two of them started to move away. The Innkeeper did not return inside his inn, however. Wally stood there in the doorway, watching the forlorn couple. His mouth was open, his brow creased with concern, his eyes filling unmistakably with tears.

Suddenly this Christmas pageant became different from all others.

"Don't go, Joseph," Wally called out. "Bring Mary back!" And Wallace Purling's face grew into a bright smile. "You can have my room."

Some people in town thought that the pageant had been ruined. Yet there were others—many, many others—who considered it the most Christmas of all Christmas pageants they had ever seen.

Dina Donohue

The Cradle

To have a child left on their doorstep just two days before Christmas was unbelievable. Over the past three years, Cedric and Mary Adamson had almost forgotten what a real Christmas was. How were they to create Christmas for an angel–faced little girl with trusting blue eyes and a halo of blond hair, a child whom they had never seen before and in all probability would never see again?

"I hope she can have a good Christmas," the young father had said. "She'll stay with you all right. She was going to spend the holidays with my brother and his wife on their farm. She's not ever seen them, so it won't make a lot of difference."

Earlier that morning, big feathery snowflakes had begun to fall, a lazy handful or two at first, then much thicker as the day wore on. By late afternoon Mary scarcely could see across the barnyard for the drifts.

"Did you see that old trailer at the foot of the hill?" Cedric asked as he stamped his snowy boots on the back porch.

"No, I didn't," Mary replied, "I haven't lifted my nose from this quilting frame all afternoon. If there's anything I like, it's quilting during a snowfall."

"Looked pretty dilapidated," Cedric said. "Like as not, they're going to wait out the storm. Can't say as I blame them. We're in for a real snow this time."

It was on the tip of Mary's tongue to say, "I always liked a white Christmas." But she didn't. *The less said, the better,* she reminded herself. She left the quilting frame and stepped over to the window.

"It worries me thinking of them spending a night like this in that contraption," she said. "Maybe you ought to invite them up here."

Mary glanced back across her shoulder at the big, black range with its crackling fire.

"If it gets too bad, they'll come up here without an invitation," Cedric said. "People like that learn to take care of themselves."

It was thirty minutes before midnight when the anxious pounding sounded on the back door. Mary awoke with a start. Cedric, lamp in hand, followed her to the kitchen. Young Bert Mannion had climbed the hill through the snowstorm to ask them to call a doctor.

"I'm scared," he admitted. "Her time isn't until next month. We thought we'd be with our folks by then. It's hard among strangers."

"Now don't you think of us as strangers," Mary told him. "At times like this, we're all friends. Cedric and I'll do anything we can to help."

"Sure, son. Just you name it." Cedric added.

The young man's face brightened. "Well, will you keep an eye on the trailer? I'm going to unhook the car and drive my wife to the hospital. And would you keep Marcia until I get back? She's three and awful good. She won't be much bother."

"Just you bring her up, and we'll look after her," Mary assured him. "And don't worry. You stay with your wife as long as you need."

Almost before they could catch their breath, Bert had returned with the little girl in his arms. Snowflakes clung to her long lashes and blue hood. She smiled at them hesitantly. In that moment it was as though Christina had never left them.

During Marcia's nap that next afternoon, Mary searched through the kitchen cabinet for her star–shaped cookie cutters. Where had she put them? She finally decided to cut the cookies out by hand, not forgetting the gingerbread man that Christina had always loved.

Christina, born after years of waiting, had died on Christmas Eve just three years ago. Cedric had never fully recovered from the shock. Even now, the sight of a Christmas tree in a store window would leave him haggard and sick, so he avoided town during the season.

Each Christmas Mary had suggested that they trim a tree and set up the little crèche in honor of the Christ Child, but her husband had steadfastly maintained that there was no room in the house for a tree.

Mary had felt the urge to lash back with "No, there's no room for a tree, or the Christ Child, or anything else—except sadness when Christmas rolls around. We can't go on living in the past, Cedric. Christina wouldn't want us to shut Christmas out of our hearts forever, nor would the Christ." But as usual, she held her peace.

Mary wondered how Cedric would hold up in this situation. She hadn't seen him since he returned to the barn after lunch, and a great knot of uneasiness had been growing in her heart for the past hour.

If only I could help him! she thought. *If he could only understand that Christmas is not Christina's day, that it belongs to Christ.*

"Auntie Mae! Auntie Mae!" Marcia's voice interrupted her musings. Wiping her hands on her apron, she turned to the child.

"Well, bless your heart," Mary said, pushing the ringlets from Marcia's forehead. "Would you like to watch me make cookies?" She lifted the child to a chair beside the table and began patting raisin buttons down the plump tummy of a gingerbread man.

"When Daddy and Mommy come back we'll have a baby, won't we?" Marcia said.

"Yes, a sweet little baby." Mary wondered how long they would keep the child's mother in the hospital, and if she would regain her strength in that drafty trailer. Perhaps they could bring her to the house—but that would be too hard on Cedric. He hadn't wanted to look at a baby since Christina died. Having Marcia here was enough.

Mary glanced toward the barn. She was almost sure Cedric would be there in his workshop where he had spent the afternoon before Christina's death. Every Christmas Eve since, he had hidden himself there to hide his grief from her.

"Will we have a Christmas tree?" Marcia asked, breaking the silence in the big kitchen. "Daddy said we could have one."

Mary turned her gaze to the cedars nestling against the hillside. "I don't know. We'll have to ask Uncle Cedric." She had hoped he would come in for his afternoon coffee, but there was no sign of him. She took their wraps from the hall tree for the snowy walk to the barn.

The scattered hay on the floor outside the workshop muffled their footsteps, but as an extra precaution she placed a finger against her lips to warn Marcia not to speak out. Quietly she tiptoed to a spot where a rotted board provided a peephole into the shop.

There was Cedric with Christina's unfinished doll cradle clutched in his hands. His knuckles stood out a polished white against the leathery brown of his skin. The cradle shook, as did his broad shoulders, and tears coursed down his cheeks. Mary closed her eyes, and a sickness she had not known in months swept over her.

The cradle! It was the cradle that had kept alive the sorrow in his heart. He had been working on it as a Christmas surprise the afternoon she had called to tell him Christina had taken a sudden turn for the worse. It had hung unfinished from the rafters ever since, except when Cedric would take it down during one of his spells of melancholy.

There had been times when Mary wished she had the courage to smash it with a hammer and burn it out of their lives forever, as she had done with the rag doll she had finished that same day. *Someday it must be destroyed or it will destroy us,* she told herself. She turned swiftly, took Marcia in her arms and hurried out of the barn.

It was time for milking when Cedric appeared at the back door looking gray and lined. "You missed your coffee," Mary told him.

"Yes," he grunted. "I was busy." He turned toward the milk pails.

"It's late, I'll help you." Mary said, reaching for her jacket and Marcia's hooded coat.

Cedric made no comment as they followed his tracks through the snow. Noting his bent shoulders beneath the blue denim windbreaker, Mary told herself, *I won't force Christmas on him, even for Marcia.* But there was a lump in her throat as she glanced down at the little girl struggling to keep up with them.

Cedric had already milked old Nell and was walking down the barn aisle with his brimming pail in one hand and a kerosene lantern in the other. Mary patted Queenie's velvet flank and rose slowly from the three-legged stool. Her breath caught in a tight knot as her husband put down his pail and turned abruptly into the workshop. Leaving Marcia to watch over her pail of milk, she hurried after him.

She paused outside the workshop, trembling with cold as she had the night Christina died. Then the chill turned to hot anger. The moment had come. She would step in there and smash the cradle to bits before his very eyes. She put the pail down and stepped soundlessly through the doorway.

Cedric's back was to her, and she might easily have taken the hammer from its place without him noticing. But in a swift spasm of contrition she knew she could not do this to him, not on Christmas Eve. Her eyes misted and she wanted to comfort him as she might a child.

She took a quick step, then froze suddenly, too amazed to move. The light from the lantern fell on the workbench, and what she saw in its glow caused her to gasp. Like one in a trance, he had reached toward the miniature cradle and was rocking it gently.

"Cedric," she cried, rushing forward and throwing her arms around him, her tears spilling down his denim sleeve. She had wanted to destroy the cradle. To put it out of their lives forever, but Cedric had found a better way of freeing them from its spell. He had fitted it with rockers and polished its rich walnut until it shone.

"The little one will want presents when she wakes on Christmas. Even the Christ Child had gifts," he said. The words spoken, a great weight seemed to slip from him. "I saw the new rag doll on your machine. That's what gave me the courage to do this."

He stared for a moment, then squared his chin firmly. "A doll and a cradle and a little one—and the peace of God in our hearts. This will be a real Christmas!"

Mary's heart soared like a bird. "I'll bring down the crèche from the attic!"

As her eyes met Cedric's she saw a man made new and strong once more. He had faced up to his sorrow. It would never possess him again. The spirit of love had triumphed over the spirit of grief. They had returned at long last to the blessed meaning of Christmas—through a child and a cradle.

Myrtle Vorst Sheppard

Beyond the Burning

Joy watched the pine logs burn side by side in the grate. Soft sighing sounds emerged, as though the two logs were gauging time, lest one should burn more quickly than the other. With a kind of morbid fascination she wondered if one might be left to grow cold alone.

It was nearly Christmas and, for the first time in all the years she could remember, there was no tree in the living room, no red and green decorations artfully placed. Even the crèche that had always signaled Advent in their home lay hidden inside its box near the mantle.

It hadn't been a conscious decision, really. But after all, there was no one but herself this year. Harold had passed away suddenly one cruelly brilliant day in July. And Janie had wed Martin Crane and gone on an extended trip to Australia. They would not be back until spring, and then perhaps only for a visit.

Jessica was finishing a term at the University of Edinburgh and would spend a late Christmas with Mom in mid–January. So three days before Christmas, Joy was all alone. Dreadfully alone.

She could have gone to her brother's in Colorado, but in some strange way she might feel even more alone. At least here she and Harold had been together—like two logs blazing companionably in growing old age.

She frowned into the mirror above the fireplace. Old age? At fifty? Really? There was still a certain comeliness about her hazel eyes and chestnut hair only mildly touched with strands of gray.

Joy turned away, suddenly tired and frightened by her uncharacteristic gloom. She thought she had worked through all that pain in the difficult months past. Friends had been supportive, good. She stooped to loosen the twine around the box. As she raised the box, she remembered how much she had been helped, how much kindness had come to her.

So what was wrong with her? Maybe it was the pressure at work. Dismally, she glanced in the direction of the coffee table. A thick folder lay at a haphazard angle where she had thrown it earlier.

Hank Collier used to be such a generous, kind employer—even giving her extra time off after Harold's death. But lately, he'd turned into some kind of ogre, taciturn and demanding.

Imagine asking for that extensive research data at three o'clock on Friday afternoon—especially at the holiday season when everyone had so much to do! Or perhaps he thought single women didn't need time to bake cookies or wrap gifts, or . . . She had only begun to learn how difficult the single life could sometimes be.

Well, she had told Hank he would have to wait—at least until Monday. She had not said it very kindly. Nor had he responded. He had looked at her with those little muscles in his jaw working, then turned on his patent-leathered heels and left the room.

"Joy to the World," she said to the image in the mirror, sensing the cruel irony of her name. She took the file to her workroom. Why not? There was nothing else to do but stare at the logs in the fireplace.

When the project was finished she got into her car, only slightly aware that a light snow was falling and that she had not taken the time for supper. She would deliver the material so Hank could have his Saturday meeting—or do whatever he planned with the file.

The Collier home on the outskirts of town was a handsome one. His father had lived there before him—and perhaps his father's father, too, who had been something of a real estate magnate in that part of the country. It certainly looked like he could afford to hire one more secretary to help with the workload.

She slammed the car door, surprised by the angry noise it made. They would probably be gathered around a fire. The children would be sitting near the tree, dreaming perhaps.

Joy knocked too loudly, wondering about the loneliness plaguing her now. Wondering if it was burning out of control. She knocked again. There was no response. Strange. She could hear a television going, and lights were blazing from the windows. Irritated, she moved around to the rear of the house. The least they could do would be to answer the door, after all the extra work she had put in.

She pressed her face against the back window. Suddenly she saw flames rising from the stove. She banged against the glass, then at the back door. Someone had obviously turned the stove up too high under a large frying pan.

A little boy streaked into the room. Then a girl, maybe twelve or so, with long dark hair streaming behind her. She put both hands to her mouth as she drew near the stove, then backed up, screaming. Joy pushed against the door with all her weight, and suddenly she was inside the room.

"The flour! Where's the flour!" she yelled. Instinctively she grabbed the largest canister on the counter near the stove and threw its entire contents over the flames.

A thunk and a hissing, and the flames became a smoking, sticky mess. Joy turned to see the young girl, white as the flour and shivering against the kitchen wall. The boy, whimpering in the doorway, ran to his sister and clung to her blue–jeaned knees.

"It's all right," Joy said gently. She put an arm around the girl's shoulders. "I'm Joy Nelson. I work for your father. I'm so glad you're all right."

The girl nodded and sniffed. "Thank—thank you," she stammered.

"Are you alone here? Where's your mother?"

"She's—sick. She's—in the hospital and Daddy—"

At that point Hank Collier rushed into the kitchen, snowflakes clinging to his hair and coat.

"Oh, Daddy!" The girl rushed to her father, who held her against his chest while his eyes searched Joy's for an explanation.

"I came to deliver the research data—the project I told you I couldn't do. I saw the grease fire from the window." She paused, seeing the mixture of pain and relief on her employer's face. Strange, she hadn't noticed those lines of worry before.

Hank Collier shook his head as he released his young daughter. "I'm very grateful," he said slowly. "I—I had to leave the children to visit Mary. My wife—" His words broke off, and he dropped down in a kitchen chair.

"Oh, Hank. I'm so sorry. I wish I had known. I would have been glad to help." Suddenly she was ashamed of herself. She should have guessed that something had been worrying him. But she hadn't been able to see beyond herself.

She began cleaning up the mess on the stove. Jenny helped, scraping flour into a paper bag, while Hank consoled the little boy on his knee.

"We had hoped Mary would be home for Christmas, but it looks like it won't happen for a while yet." He looked off somewhere into space as he spoke, and his voice was heavy with sadness.

"Daddy, can we get our Christmas tree now? Can we?" The child pulled impetuously at his daddy's face.

Hank sighed deeply, his blue eyes closing briefly in concentration, or maybe in desperate prayer.

"Why not let me help? I could take the children shopping. I—know how difficult it must have been for you." She paused, noticing for the first time how young and vulnerable he seemed. He was wearing mismatched socks—one navy blue with ribs and the other smooth and black. She smiled, hoping he understood how sorry she was for her earlier lack of understanding.

"I know I owe you an apology," he said in a low, weary voice. "You—and everybody else in the office. I guess I let my problems get the upper hand and I—"

"Believe me, I understand. Listen," she began gently. "I have a freezer full of Christmas cookies that I baked out of habit. But now I don't know what to do with them."

"You have gingerbread men?" the little boy asked with wide eyes.

"The biggest gingerbread men with the most frosting you ever saw," she said, feeling the wonderment of Christmas like a meteor rising in her soul. And to think she had almost let it all pass her by, like so much smoke. Beyond the burning of her own grief she had finally felt the pain of another. Strange what warmth and light were touched off in the shared flame.

Lt. Colonel Marlene Chase

Spring

Everything that's new has bravely surfaced,

teaching us to breathe;

What was frozen through is newly purposed,

turning all things green;

And so it is with You, and how You make me new

with every season's change,

So it will be, as You are re-creating me.

I Am the Wind

He was eight years old, with big blue eyes that saw everything with wonder. The day was warm that May, and his mother had said he could go barefoot! His shoes flew off—and his toes curled down into the sun–warmed earth. His toes became ten funnels of feeling sucking the warm up inside him.

Just then, the fragrant plum blossoms shed their snowy petals across the orchard fence. He scampered toward the scented breeze and, with his toes, bent the tender grass where drifting petals alighted in a creamy foam.

He darted through the wide boards of the fence, running toward the *chug–chug* of the tractor. His father, a big man with freckles, waved to him—boy's eyes and man's eyes cut from the same piece of blue.

The boy had two delicious choices—walk in the fresh furrows, shiny and smoothly new, or walk in the soft squishy loam, leaving tracks like a tiger cat. He got sidetracked making the big decision, enchanted by a fat grubworm. As the boy prodded it with his toes, a rooster with a perky red comb ran up and gobbled the worm. The boy flapped his wings and crowed like the rooster.

Wind blew the boy's short red–gold hair. He tried to capture the wind with his fingers. But the wind blew on. He looked longingly after it, trying to see what wind looks like. But all he saw were ripples in the lake, as the plum blossoms swayed—touched by the same invisible force. More creamy petals floated on the wind, so lazy they couldn't seem to make up their minds where to fall.

The boy threw his head back, inhaling deeply. He wished his nostrils were bigger so they could smell more good smells. What did fresh earth have in it that made it smell so good?

The sun felt friendly on top of his head. His breakfast left a glow inside his stomach. He wished—how he wished—he were big enough to drive the tractor! Someday.

"Chug–chug," he said, running down the fresh furrow. He tugged on the imaginary steering wheel of the pretend tractor. But he gave it up. It wasn't the same as a real steering wheel. He would have to grow.

Was it really true, if a boy ate up the bacon rinds on his plate, that would make his whiskers grow? Why did Dad grin when he said it?

The boy ran down the furrow, leaping wildly. He changed into a deer, pursued by hunters. *Zing* went the bullet! He fell full length, as though he had no bones, feeling the rising dampness of the ground and the layer of sun on top. His hands came up, both fists filled with dirt. He squeezed the fresh earth. How can dirt be dirty, like under his nails, but look so clean and shiny new?

As though using a microscope, he examined intently each grain of soil. The fresh earth crumbled and fell apart, rolling. Where did the grains come from, so many? What made them stick together? What made them fall apart? Dirt was like the petals of the plum blossoms. It kept changing into something new. *Why?*

The boy lay flat on his back, staring into the bluest of skies, enchanted by the immensity of his new discovery—the earth upon which he lay. The grains of dirt went on and on, touching other grains, but each one is its own grain. This field touching the other field. On and on—into town, under the rivers, under the ocean, touching China, touching Australia, coming back again, touching him from the other side! The earth was too big for him.

And the sky looked even bigger.

What made it blue? Where did the blue go at night? What made the stars pop out after dark? He watched a bird fly from its nest in the plum tree. The bird grew smaller, got lost in the blue.

Away up—high, high, almost above the blue—a lone buzzard circled. It went round and round like a merry–go–round that didn't know how to stop. Watching it, the boy became the bird.

He could feel the wind in his feathers—the world beneath was his toy! He could light on any spot he liked. He could feel the rubber–like covering of his small–boned bird legs. His sharp claws relaxed, touching his bird body.

Wind flowed over and under him like soft water. He swam through the wind. He was a feather, then a cork, bobbing, bobbing. He rolled over, instantly becoming a boy again. Alert. Alive.

Spot, the plump, half–grown pup, began to chase a young rabbit across the rows of freshly plowed earth, yelping as if angry bees were stinging him. The rabbit ran through the orchard fence, crossed the drainage ditch, and disappeared inside a tangled thicket of last year's vines and leaves.

Spot returned, panting, looking into the boy's eyes. *He had a head start on me!* Spot's eyes said, seeking sympathy. The boy patted Spot's head. Instantly, Spot was freed from guilt. He ran toward a gopher hole, scratching energetically. Fresh dirt clung to the tip of his moist nose. Spot drank the clean air, boastful. *It was just a little old piddling rabbit, anyway. But I am a mighty hunter, just watch my technique with this gopher.* (Dig, dig, snort, dig, dig.)

The boy forgot the rabbit, forgot Spot, forgot the vastness of the earth and sky. He contemplated his dirt–stained feet. It had been less than ten minutes since he had shed his socks and shoes! Where had the wonderful, new feeling gone? Already his feet were getting used to going naked. He frowned, annoyed that it should be so. He wanted to keep the I'm–going–barefoot experience new and shining. *How can you keep a good thing new? How do you keep a feeling from changing?*

I am not me, he told himself. *I am ten little people. I am the Ten Toes Brothers, and this is our first fine holiday! All we have to do is feel the warmth and the sun and the sand. We'll just go on feeling and feeling.* He frowned again. *How do you go on and on doing the same thing and never getting tired? How do you make a good feeling last?*

He then had to ask himself a serious question.

Suppose I did drive the tractor, not just pretend drive. After I drove all around the farm, would the new feeling wear off?

How do you pickle up the good, like plum preserves in a jar?

The boy looked earnestly at the plum tree. Its blossoms were snow white. But the petals kept falling. Pretty soon the tree would put forth baby leaves. Only they didn't stay little. They became bigger leaves. Then later little green plums grew beneath their leaves. Then bigger green plums. Then yellow plums, then pinky–red, then deep red. *Plop!* Into a pie or a basket.

Everything gets old. Everything. Me. Spot. Someday I'll be a big boy. Then a man. Then an old man. With white whiskers, probably.

"Spot," folks would say, "he's an old dog now." Good old Spot.

"No!" he shouted loudly. "I'm barefoot! It's new. It's going to stay new!" He felt a trifle silly because he knew—something inside him knew—shouting was not going to change it.

Slowly he stopped feeling sorry for himself as a smell—a wonderful, delicious smell—made his nostrils grow wide in anticipation.

Bread!

He sat up, then ran toward the kitchen like a streak. His mother was setting three golden brown loaves of yeast bread on the kitchen table. Their eyes met.

"Do I have to wait?" asked the boy.

"Well—" His mother gave him a smile. She turned around for a hot pad and broke one of the loaves in two. He watched the tantalizing waves rush out and hit his hungry stomach. His mom set strawberry preserves, butter, a knife and the broken bread on a serving tray.

"Don't forget Spot," she said, as if Spot would allow that to happen!

The boy stopped halfway through the kitchen door. His freckled smile was special. "I like you, Mom," he said.

"How about that, Spot?" the boy said later, chewing dreamily. They dropped a few crumbs. That's how they met the ant family.

He didn't mean to forget about how good it is to be barefoot. It was just that he got so interested in watching the ants that the wonder of going barefoot got crowded out. Changes. Everything changes.

Where do they go, those busy little critters who live in the ground? What do they find down there? Do they have private tunnels like highways? Do they have telephone lines? If not, how does the word get around so fast? Look at all these others. Who told them it was bread day?

He meant to walk to the other side of the field where his father had stopped the tractor while he talked with a neighbor. But he got to thinking about the wind.

If you shut your eyes tight, if you listen hard, the wind blows down inside you. The wind goes under your skin. It travels up through your fingernails and out through your toes. Your body is like a big sponge! It seeps in the wind, just like a sponge soaks up water. And when you let your breath out slowly—you become the wind!

The boy sank down on the soft, plowed, warm earth. He drew Spot tightly against him, both of them full of yeast bread. The sun warmed them. For a moment, he became a loaf of warm bread, yeast rising, like when the oven is turned to low. He was a loaf of bread baked by the sun. Slow–baked. It was like he was dreaming, but he was not dreaming. He was being.

He was the Ten Toes Brothers. He was the butterfly on a nearby clover blossom. He was the plum blossoms. All twisting and turning, in love with the sun. He was the little rabbit, leaping, frightened, running for his life from Spot. He was Spot, chasing the rabbit. He was the gopher, groping under the earth. But he was also change.

He looked like a boy lying motionless in the sun. But that was just the outside part. The inside part was that old buzzard, playing merry–go–round, getting skydust blue on his feathers. He was the warm melted gold of the sun that made the plants grow, that created change, that made the plums ripe. He was the sun's gilded paint, spraying goldshine.

He was warmth. He was understanding. He was life.

He was also the wind.

Kermit Shelby

Flower on the Sidewalk

Meg MacDonald vigorously swept her veranda with an enthusiasm undiminished in fifty years of ownership. With a veteran's touch she flicked at the grit, following it down the freshly painted, wooden steps, along the garden path and across the hot sidewalk.

Resting her hands on the broom, she appraised her two–story, stone house, well–preserved by her Sam . . . until two years ago. Involuntarily she squared her shoulders—a habit from childhood of carrying her five feet, nine inches straight and tall, now despite the wrinkles and white hair.

Meg bent to pick up a chunk of insulbrick, turning it over in her hand and then looking toward the next cottage. Every day there seemed to be a little more debris in her front yard. Every time she glanced over at the cottage nextdoor, she noticed a bit more of the weather–beaten clapboard was exposed.

She remembered what a nice house it had been, way back in Mrs. Baxter's day, when Sam and she had bought their own home. Mrs. Baxter had laughed at them—just married, and buying a seven–room house! There had been wry comments about the size of the family they would need to fill it. Bigger houses were family homes back then, not hacked–up into cramped apartments.

Well, she sighed, she and Sam had filled it all right. And now they'd all gone, even the grandchildren. Everyone had scattered! Other children now played in the neighborhood, undisciplined and often unfriendly.

As she resumed her sweeping, Meg peered at the old, wrecked sedan from the corner of her eye. It had been abandoned in the lane between their two houses, right under her dining room window.

How Sam would have hated that!

Around the wreck lay other junk—a smashed playpen, handlebars from a bike, fencing torn down and thrown in a heap, bits of the grand maple tree broken by swinging boys.

And those unbearable windows of the cottage, opaque with grime, with narrow plastic drapes crazily dragged across. She often wondered about the inside.

The new girl was on the steps again, but Meg always looked away quickly and kept to her sweeping. Between thirteen and sixteen years old, Meg guessed, sallow–complexioned with masses of untidy hair. Dirty, tight shorts were fixed on her thin frame with a safety pin.

Meg approached the point between the two houses where she always felt the urge to go on, past the frightful place, just for once to see the whole sidewalk spruced up!

Equally strong, yet strangely inhibited, was her desire to get acquainted with this forlorn figure. She'd heard her name was Patty, but she could never tell whether the girl was looking at her or not from beneath all that hair.

Finally, the urge to keep sweeping overpowered her, and she just made the dust fly until she was directly in line with the neighbors' steps. Then she looked up at Patty again, and this time she offered a greeting. "Hi."

The girl's response was inaudible, unsmiling, but Meg saw the lips move, and so she swept another two feet.

"Excuse me, won't you," Meg said, finally acknowledging her own diligent behavior. "I just can't resist cleaning up."

Patty scooted her feet and rested her chin on the other hand.

"Looks so much nicer after it's been swept," Meg began again.

Patty moved her head slightly, then lifted her thin shoulders and let them fall again. "What's the difference?" Her voice was flat.

"Why, it makes all the difference in the world."

"What difference?"

"It makes people feel better."

"It doesn't make me feel better."

Meg flicked at a pebble as she began to respond but stared back in dismay, instead, at the empty steps. Patty had gone inside.

Immediately from the apartment came a howl of rage trailing off into a pitiful wail.

Meg flung down her broom and took off with more haste than dignity over the dandelion patch and up the rickety steps. When she pushed open the rotted screen door she smelled the scorching.

Patty stood over an ironing board clutching something white and crumpled. Blinking at Meg through her tears, she babbled something about leaving the iron to warm and the dog flipping the cord.

Meg took the material from Patty's hands, shook it and held it up. It was a simple, white dress with an iron–shaped piece burned clean out near the back hemline.

"I—I have to wear it tonight," whimpered Patty.

Something suddenly clicked with Meg. "Graduation? Your eighth grade graduation?"

"Tonight," Patty nodded miserably.

Folding the dress carefully, Meg hung it over her arm. "Come along to my place," she said calmly. "We'd best get busy right away."

Patty drew the back of her hand across her eyes. "Y'mean it'll fix for tonight?"

Like watching the sun peep through after a shower, thought Meg.

"I often thought of throwing out this stuff." Meg laughed softly as she rummaged through the old chest. "Thought my patching days were over."

Patty looked around. "Big house. Guess you had lots of kids."

Meg straightened up and held a piece of material against the damaged dress. "Guess you could call six a big family these days."

Heads together, they pinned on the patch at the big kitchen table.

"There!" Meg drew up a chair to the sewing machine. "If my hands are steady enough, no one'll ever know the difference."

"I like to sew," Patty said quietly. "But we got no machine at home."

Meg quickly relinquished the chair. "I used to be an expert on graduation dresses—long ago." She heaved a little sigh.

Patty sewed quietly for a minute, then snipped at the thread and drew out the repair. "None of them living near you?"

"Not a one!"

"It used to be nice when our Gran was around."

"Don't you visit her?" asked Meg.

"Too far away." A wistful note had crept into Patty's voice as she carefully studied the patch on her dress. Then suddenly she burst out bitterly, "That's the trouble—always leaving people behind."

"There were others?" Meg asked, gently, tactfully.

"My friends," Patty swallowed hard. "A family's got to move when the landlord says."

Meg felt uncomfortable. Carrying her own sense of pride like a banner, she had never unexpectedly marched onto another's. But concern, she felt, sometimes came first. So she asked, "Why would the landlord do that?"

The girl's head was down, straggly hair concealing her face. "He would say we weren't keeping his property good. That's after the neighbors had let into him."

Meg felt her scalp prickle. It was the same kind of shock she'd felt the time little Mary Jane had prayed, "And please help Mummy not be too pure and holy—like Helen's mummy says."

"But I thought your mum went to work?"

"Yes! Now she does, and she's always tired. She says if you got nothing and nobody, you can't do nothing with a place."

Patty suddenly gathered up the white dress and started for the door, but Meg quickly laid a hand on her arm and drew her towards the piano.

"My dear, when I came to Canada I was just your age. I came with the orphans."

"Orphans?" Patty looked at her quickly, curiously.

Meg nodded. "I had nothing and nobody." For a moment she was serious, thoughtful, then lifting her hand to indicate a row of pictures on the piano, "Look, my graduates," she said proudly, radiantly.

But the spark of interest had already left Patty's face and, barely glancing at the row of smiling faces, she turned again to the door.

"Better hurry. Got to do something with my hair."

"Your mum will be so proud," Meg hurried after her. "And she'll not even notice the patch."

"My mum won't even be there! She's on late shift!"

After Patty had gone, Meg returned to her cherished photos, lifting them one by one and gazing at each a little sadly at first, then thoughtfully. Where had Rod stored the family camera and flash when he had brought the grandchildren to visit last winter?

Meg spent much of her time before the graduation ceremony practicing with the camera. When Patty stepped up to receive the familiar little beribboned diploma later that evening, Meg was there.

Although Meg half–heartedly flicked the broom over the sidewalk every day, it was more than a week later before she glimpsed Patty and beckoned her into the house.

"I've something to show you." Gently smiling but quite excited, Meg again drew Patty over to the piano. She watched the girl's eyes travel along the line of photos, then widen and fill with tears when she saw herself in the white dress.

"And here," Meg held out another photo of Patty at graduation. "Here's one to send to your gran."

Meg just had time to place the photo into Patty's limp hand and close the thin fingers over it before the girl suddenly turned, bolted for the door and was gone without a word.

It was days before Meg saw her again. She waited and wondered as she tended the back garden, where those stubborn weeds had sprung up again. Once, she held up an unkempt, foot–high daisy to admire. It had stood condemned as a weed, a threat to gardening law and order.

But what of people, Meg thought. You couldn't label people that way. They all had to put down roots in order to live—in a spiritual sense that is. To blossom they had to be wanted and loved some place. And what about those of us who are the transplants?

Carelessness, as Meg well knew, killed off all but the hardiest plants. But what of Patty? Was it already too late for her?

Meg's answer came unexpectedly the next time she happened to be adjusting the front drapes.

Patty was out there giving the sidewalk the most vigorous sweeping it had had in many a year!

Nell Miller

Just for Today

"It was such fun picking these pretty flowers, Grandma. I have never seen so many colors! The whole field looked like my box of crayons had spilled all over!"

On and on she chattered, asking question after question. Most of them were impossible to answer, but I nodded and smiled anyway. It was so good having her here with me. She reminds me so much of her mother.

"You know, Tish, when your Mommy was a little girl, she and I used to go to that very same field to pick flowers."

She looked up at me, excitement dancing in her eyes. "I bet Mommy will just love this bouquet when she comes home from the hospital, 'specially when she finds out we got them from her favorite field."

"I'm sure she will, dear." My body stood here arranging flowers with my granddaughter, but my mind traveled across the miles to the hospital where Ginny would be preparing to come home. It wasn't really a joyful homecoming, though. When cancer takes its final toll, they send you home for only one reason. How do you explain that to a six–year–old? Her young voice brought me back.

"Grandma, isn't it true that God knows everything?"

"Yes honey, He does, but why do you ask?"

"Does He know we picked these flowers for Mommy?"

"Yes."

"Did He know last year we were going to do it?"

"Well, I guess so. Why?"

A satisfied smile appeared on her face. "Then He grew them extra pretty for us!"

Her little hands worked eagerly to arrange them as I had taught her, carefully putting brilliant colors in the right spot to offset the white daisies.

"Grandma, am I being a stumper?"

"What?"

"A stumper. You know, Daddy says I'm a stumper."

"Lands alive, child, whatever makes you ask that?"

"'Cause you look funny, like you don't know what to say to me."

"Well, I—"

"And another thing. Why do you look so sad, when Mommy is coming home? She's been away so long. Aren't you happy she's coming home?"

"Of course, sweetheart. It's just that, well …" I sat down, turned her around and took her tiny hands in mine. Brushing a golden curl from her forehead, I said, "Tish, you do understand that Mommy is still very sick, don't you?"

"Yes, Daddy told me."

"That's why I'm a little sad. I just wish Mommy was all better."

"Why?"

"Well, because I love her." She stopped fussing with my fingers and looked straight at me. Her next words startled me beyond description.

"Then let Jesus have her."

"Tish, whatever do you mean?"

My voice must have revealed my bewilderment, for she crawled up into my lap and began to explain to me in a matter–of–fact way that made me feel like a child.

"Daddy and I talk to Jesus about Mommy all the time. Then we talk to each other. Last night, Daddy told me how very much Jesus loves Mommy and how sorry He is she hurts so much from being sick. She hurts lots, Grandma."

"Yes, I know, honey." Tears began to form in my eyes.

"Well, Jesus can take that hurt away if Mommy goes to live with Him in Heaven. Daddy and I decided we love Mommy enough to let

Jesus have her. Besides, that way she can get things ready for us." She grinned. "You know how she's always worrying about such things. One thing, though, Mommy mustn't know. It's to be a surprise when Jesus comes for her."

I could control the tears no longer, and they spilled down my cheeks. I felt ashamed and naked, with no place to hide my grief.

She spoke again with amazing insight. "Oh, Grandma, I cry sometimes too." She jumped down and placed a bright pink field rose in the vase.

"Look, Grandma, look at the pretty flowers. Flowers are for being happy; happy that Mommy is coming home, happy that the sun is shining, happy to be here on the farm, happy that God loves us— happy just for today."

I hugged her much too tight, and she squealed. "You're right, sweetheart. Let's take the flowers out on the porch where Mommy can see them when she drives up."

The sky was blue, the air was fresh, and Ginny was on her way home. I looked heavenward and sighed, "Thank you, Jesus, just for today!"

Major Dorothy Hitzka

The Future Father

Jim Riley would have rated himself a good husband, father and provider. He owed no money but the mortgage, neither gambled, smoked nor drank, was faithful to his wife and considerate of his in–laws, and not only attended church on Sunday but also taught a Bible class.

He certainly couldn't say the same thing about Hal Bromley across the street. Jim didn't know whether Hal was faithful or not, or whether Hal's church attendance matched his own, but he knew for a fact that Hal owed not only on his mortgage but also on his car and stereo, and that he had borrowed on his life insurance to take his family out West the summer before.

When Jim Riley was out attacking the crabgrass, Hal was off to the park to jog with his son. When a storm blew down trees in both the Riley and Bromley yards, Jim had a man come out the next day to chop his up and haul it away, while the Bromley tree stayed down for six months so the kids could play on it.

"No get–up–and–go," Jim said to his wife once as they watched Hal Bromley sprawled in a lawn chair, his kids tumbling about him on the grass. Jim, on the other hand, had organized his children into a window–washing team and hoped to have the lower windows done by afternoon.

Some people just didn't understand about planning and organizing their time, he decided. The Bromleys, for instance, had made that trip out West when their youngest was only four. All that time and expense, and what was the kid going to remember of the Grand Canyon when he was older?

And as for work around the house, well, you had to keep up with the seasons. If you wanted a good crop of grass in summer, you had to sow your seed the previous fall. If you didn't get the windows washed in the spring, you'd have them to do in the sweltering summer heat. Life required a plan. It had regulations. If you wanted to live well, you had to play by the rules—that's all there was to it.

It bothered Jim at times that Gerry and Gus preferred to play at the Bromley house, especially during that summer when the tree fell down. Once when he saw Gretchen, his five–year–old, sitting beside Hal Bromley on the lawn chair chattering away, he called her home on some pretext and was ashamed, and a little baffled, at his reaction.

But today was Friday: It was the end of a hard week, and it was also Jim Riley's birthday. Marge had baked the traditional coconut cake, and the kids had spent the hour before dinner wrapping their handmade creations and composing little verses on folded sheets of paper. Jim decided not to think about the Bromleys or the grass, which needed to be mowed. He looked around the dining room after dinner and took stock of the scene. Such a devoted family, Jim noted with satisfaction. And why not? Didn't he deserve it? *What you sow, that you shall also reap* . . .

It was a good celebration. The children hung about his chair and asked him to read their verses aloud, enjoying the fact that a time had been set aside for them to be together.

"I love birthdays!" Gretchen said, snuggling up against him. "I love your birthday most of all."

"My birthday?" Jim asked his daughter. "Why, I would think you wouldn't want to see your dad turning into an old man. "

Gretchen turned and faced him. "Oh, no! I can't wait until you're a grandfather!"

"A grandfather!" said Marge from across the table. "Why would you be excited about that?"

"Because then he wouldn't go to work anymore, and he'd have time to play with me, and he wouldn't have to mow the grass or go to meetings—just like Grandpa."

The older children shrieked with merriment.

"Gretchen, you dummy! When Dad's a grandfather, you'll be all grown up!" Gus said, doubling over with laughter.

Jim stared at his daughter—and she stared back—with a hurt, resentful look in her eyes.

"It'll be too late then," she said and went back to her chair at the table, silently finishing her cake.

A nerve had been touched, a nerve long–ignored. How long had she been waiting for his time and attention? Ever since she was born? How long had Gus and Gerry been waiting for him to give of himself before they had just given up? How easily he could understand their excitement now when they drove to Grandpa's every summer, how obvious their delight in the house across the street.

"Tomorrow maybe," he had said when Gus and Gerry asked him to play badminton with them, and the next day it rained.

"When you're older," he had told them when they wanted to go fishing at the pond, and the following year the pond was filled in.

"Some other time," he had told Gretchen once when she wanted to read her first book to him. She never asked again.

Not now, later—not today—ask me tomorrow—next summer, perhaps. The list of delays went on and on.

When Gretchen was a mother herself, and her own children played on his lap, would she look at him with those same resentful eyes, remembering the days he never had time for her?

"You've given me a good party," he told the three children before him, "and I really appreciate it. Now it's my turn. You save tomorrow afternoon for me, and we'll all do a surprise together—something very special. And for the rest of the evening, let's just read books together and tell jokes and help Mommy with the dishes—things we haven't done for a long time."

It was unheard of!

The air was filled with delighted shrieks and yelps and guesses as to what the surprise might be. Gretchen stood looking at him in wonder, and Jim grabbed her and hugged her hard.

He didn't even know yet what the surprise would be, but he'd think of something. And he was going to think of a way to keep this new relationship going with his family. It would mean a different lifestyle, he knew. It would mean that good times were now more important than crabgrass, that the present was every bit as precious as the future. It would mean that Jim Riley was going to look more and more like Hal Bromley as the months went by, but he'd do it. He had only this one chance at fatherhood now, not tomorrow.

And with that, he returned Marge's smile, cut himself some more cake, and dug in.

Phyllis Reynolds Naylor

A Time to Let Go

Harry Kobert woke up that Sunday morning with the feeling that there was something important he had to do. He didn't know what it was but was quite sure it had nothing to do with weeding the tulip bed or shining his shoes or getting to church on time. This was something else. Something new.

It happened in the middle of the night. It seemed that somehow, as he slept, a metamorphosis of sorts had taken place, that he had lived through one life cycle and started another as something or somebody else. Weird. Really weird.

It must have been something he dreamed, he decided, as he made his coffee and waited for the rest of the family to wake up. Ramona would be down soon to make the raisin buns they often had on Sunday morning. Then Doug would be down, looking as though he had grown another two inches overnight. Home from college during his first year, Doug was growing so rapidly that . . . Suddenly Harry knew that the feeling he couldn't quite place was connected somehow to Doug.

What had been on his mind just before he fell asleep last night? Maybe he could think of it that way. Did Doug need a haircut? Too late to make him get one now. Shaving? Was the kid shaved properly? Was he remembering to get that little tuft that always stuck out under the chin? Maybe that was it.

Harry stirred his coffee. No, that wasn't it. Something else. How was Doug's driving? Maybe Harry had thought to take a tour that afternoon with Doug at the wheel, making sure he didn't ride the clutch or make a rolling stop or gun the accelerator. Or maybe he had planned to sit down with the boy and work out a budget for his expenses and see how he was spending his money.

All at once, Harry knew. The feeling or the dream or whatever it was hit him right between the eyes. What Harry was planning to do was to *not do* any of the above!

But this was impossible! The kid was only eighteen! He'd only been away from home since September. He was still wet behind the ears. The hair that he never seemed to shave off below the chin was fuzz, not stubble.

Then Harry remembered the dream. It seemed that he and his son had been flying an airplane. For weeks they had been flying, years even. Harry had told him about lift and thrust and drag and gravity, about ailerons, air streams, and turbulent flow. He had demonstrated banking the plane and turning and taking off and landing. He had explained the instrument panel and radar and all the safety measures. But he had never let the boy fly the plane himself.

And then, all of a sudden, Harry had found himself unable to move, inexplicably paralyzed.

"Take over, Doug!" he had cried out. "Get us safely down!" But the boy had panicked and said, "I can't, Dad. I don't know how! I never had any practice!"

That was it. That was a dream to end all dreams. That was why he had awakened in a cold sweat and tossed around for an hour before he had drifted off again.

But that dream had characterized their relationship perfectly— instructions, advice, suggestions, rules . . . "So you won't make the same mistakes I made." How often Harry had said those words! How tired Doug must have been of hearing them.

When you came right down to it, Harry thought, what was wrong with making a few mistakes? Why had he always felt he had to budget the kid's allowance for him or he would blow it all the first day? Why not let his son have the experience of spending the money wisely, or unwisely, and taking the consequences? Why had Harry always insisted on helping choose Doug's baseball glove or running shoes or bicycle helmet? Just wanting to make sure he gets his money's worth. But what was wrong with letting him find out some things for himself?

Harry wasn't going to be around forever. It was spring. It was time the chicks came out of the shell. It was time for shoving baby birds out of the nest. It was a time for letting go, for watching new shoots spring up, new wings being tested. It ought to have been done years ago, but better now than never.

"Morning, Dad," Doug said at the table when breakfast was served. "Ah! Raisin rolls! I knew you'd make 'em, Mom!"

"So nice to have you home," Ramona said. "Such a beautiful Sunday, too. What are your plans after church, Doug?

"Oh, I'd like to see all my friends—find out who's home—just shoot the breeze. Thought I'd call Bill, see if he still has his old car."

Harry cleared his throat and tried to sound casual. "You can take ours if you like, Doug. I'm sure I can trust you with it."

There was silence all around.

"Come again?" said Doug.

Harry shrugged. "You've got your license. If you'd like to use our car, you can."

"Well, I imagine you'd get sort of bored, Dad, listening to us talk."

"I wasn't planning to go along."

"Hey, thanks! Sure, I'd like to use it!"

It was a small start—a first step. Kind of like adjusting to fatherhood all over again, but it was fathering of a different sort.

Harry let Doug drive to church and resisted all the impulses to give directions and suggestions. He sat beside his son in the pew and resisted telling Doug it would look better if he did not sit with one shoe resting on top of the other. He did not nudge him when Doug made a goof during the responsive reading or correct his pronunciation when they talked with friends after the service.

And that afternoon when he handed Doug the keys to the car, he did not add the advice "drive carefully," as though they were magic words that would protect him somehow.

There was no protective bubble, no magic, no words at all that would guarantee his son a long, happy and successful life. Harry could only hope and trust and show confidence and love.

And that was a good beginning for spring.

Phyllis Reynolds Naylor

I Love You, Mom

Abbie awoke, opened her eyes and immediately closed them to keep out the brilliant sunlight in the room. She turned her head to squint at the bed beside her. It was empty.

"Beth?" she called out. No answer, but from the shower came Beth's high-pitched voice, murdering another beautiful aria. Abbie grimaced and flung her pillow over her head.

Abbie Harper and Beth Moran were roommates, seniors at the University Hospital in Coral Gables, Florida, and very close friends since being assigned together during their freshman year.

Soon a carrot-red mop of hair, wreathed in steam, peered around the corner of the bathroom doorway. "Well, its about time you're awake, you old lazybones. C'mon, it's a fantastic day. It's our day off and it's Sunday. Let's get an early start for the beach."

Abbie glanced at her watch and gasped. She jumped out of bed and headed for the bathroom. "Why didn't you wake me?"

"Like I said, dumdum, it's our day off. What say we bypass this institutional food and treat ourselves to a decent breakfast for a change? And then we'll go on down to the beach to work on our tans." She examined her face in the mirror with disgust. "Yuk! I must have doubled the number of freckles since my last day off." She stopped as she glanced at her friend in the mirror.

Abbie was biting her lip. "But I thought we were going to church this morning. It's Mother's Day, remember? Do we have time to go to breakfast before church? Later, we can go to—"

Beth's face dropped. "We'll talk after you come out from your shower." She brushed her hair, frowning into the mirror. Why had she promised Abbie she would go to church? And today, of all days—

Mother's Day! Her frown deepened as she glared at the closed door of the bathroom. And Abbie, of all people! Why would she want to go to church today?

Abbie emerged from the steaming room, her hair wrapped in a large terrycloth towel, her frayed robe tied tightly around her waist. She was humming to herself.

Beth pretended to concentrate on buffing her nails. "Ah, Abbie? I know what I said yesterday, but that promise was made before the hectic day in emergency, before that terrible accident and all those fractures. Honestly, I'm zapped."

Abbie smiled. "Tell me about it! My feet are still burning from all that running around. And my ears! Those stethoscopes."

"All the more reason to seek relaxation, kiddo."

Abbie studied her roommate closely. "Beth, if you don't want to go to church, just say so. I understand—"

Suddenly Beth spun around on the stool, "No, you don't understand at all! Don't patronize me, Abbie. All you know about me is that I was raised by my grandmother, nothing more. But you! What about your own circumstances? Raised in a children's home, rejected by your entire family. Honestly, I don't understand you at all, Abbie, I really don't."

Something like a shadow of pain touched Abbie's brown eyes. She struggled with her next words. "I—I didn't mean to sound patronizing, Beth. I'm sorry. Maybe if I explain something to you, you can see this from my perspective. After I'm finished, and if you still feel this way, I won't say another word, I promise. Is it a deal?"

Beth sat at the edge of her bed and studied the depressively dull gray carpet with its faded yellow flowers. With reluctance, she nodded.

Abbie began. "Several years ago, when I found myself wallowing in self–pity, a wonderful woman told me something so profound that it took me a long time to really get it. She quoted something from the Bible, Psalm 27:10: *When my father and my mother forsake me, then the Lord will take me up.* I remember the time I really understood the meaning of those words. From that day on, I was never alone again."

Abbie continued to dress for church as she spoke. "A person should have to earn the privilege to be called *mother.* Think about it— There are all the surrogate parents, all the adoptive parents and step–parents. They are not easy jobs. And there are the excellent teachers of this world, and what about the foster mothers? And the grandparents, of course. Do you know what all these people have in common? The common denominator? One very simple but vital thing—love. Love, Beth, not duty."

Slowly, Beth raised her head and looked at her friend. "I get it, I think. You mentioned grandparents for my sake, didn't you?"

Abbie grinned and nodded. "When I think of Mother's Day, I think of only one person in the world that I have called *mother.* She's the superintendent of the children's home where I grew up, Mary Allen."

Beth began to get ready for church as she listened.

Abbie continued, "A few years ago, I didn't know where my life was heading. I had no ambition, no purpose, no aspirations, no goals. I was wandering around trying to 'find myself'—What a cop–out!

"Mom Allen knew me better than I knew myself, and she set me straight. She took me aside, and we had a long conversation. It was an eye–opening experience, but it was so important to me."

Abbie stopped, took a deep breath, and continued. "She actually listened to me. She listened to what I had to say, and from our conver-sation, she could tell what my goals were. She guided my life.

"And here I am today, ready to graduate from nurse's training, studying for my state boards— 'a person with a goal'! Thanks to Mom Allen. But you know something? I'm also a person who'll never feel alone, and that is thanks to the Bible verse I quoted earlier."

They ate a hasty breakfast in the hospital cafeteria, and Beth drove to church. As they walked from the parking lot, Beth noticed several people still lined up outside.

"What gives? Why is there a line? Why doesn't the crowd get in out of this hot sun?"

"Oh, today is carnation day. Wearing a carnation is an honorary gesture to all the mothers of the world," Abbie explained.

Beth felt uneasy. "Why didn't you tell me about this? I don't care for this idea at all. I won't—" She was appalled at herself. "I mean—I don't have to accept the flower, do I?"

"No, of course not. Really, Beth, it's no big deal. Just walk on by." Abbie reached out and accepted the fresh, sweet–scented carnation and pinned it to her dress.

Beth hissed in Abbie's ear, "Are you mad?! Your mother deserted you! How could you wear that thing?"

"Didn't you hear anything I said back in the room? Weren't you listening at all?"

And like a bolt of lightning, the impact of Abbie's conversation hit Beth! Quickly she plucked a flower out of the box. Before Abbie could say another word, Beth grinned sheepishly and said, "It's in honor of my *grandmother,* of course."

The transformation from blinding Florida sun into the darkness of the church made both girls hesitate until their eyes could adjust to the interior of the room. Then suddenly Abbie's face was wreathed in a smile. She waved happily to a crowd of children.

"See that woman over there with the beautiful silvery hair, the rosy cheeks, the twinkling blue eyes? The woman with a smile that lights up the world? The one with all those kids?"

Beth followed Abbie's gaze. "Who is she? And where did all those kids come from? There must be fifty hanging onto her."

"That's Mary Allen." She glanced at her friend and grinned at the expression on Beth's face. "You guessed it. She's my mother. And every child here today will honor her, including me. All forty–six kids have adopted her and call her *mother.*"

Abbie grabbed Beth's hand and flew down the aisle. When she reached Mary Allen, she leaned forward and gave the older woman a big hug and a kiss on the cheek.

"Happy Mother's Day, Mom. I love you very much."

Elizabeth Stevens Fender

How Love Is

The first time I saw Jannie, I thought she must be someone else. "Hello," she said. "Are you Mrs. McArthur?" Her voice was like water bubbling over rocks in a mountain stream—fresh and clear. "I was told to ask for you," she said. "I'm Jannie Foster."

"Well, hello," I said. "Yes, I'm Mrs. McArthur. And we've been expecting you." I hoped that I sounded as though I really meant it. But she didn't look like a student teacher to me. Maybe it was that she seemed so young. And there was a kind of delicacy about her. I began to wonder, almost immediately, how long she would last. The full semester, I hoped. She would be expected to stay that long.

"I hope you're going to like it here," I told her. "It's an excellent place to get experience in teaching special education. We have a little of everything. Some kids with mental retardation, some with learning disabilities, others with a combination of emotional and physical difficulties, too."

"I'm especially interested in working with students with developmental delays," Jannie said. Then she caught her breath a little. "I just can't quite believe this, you know. All of a sudden, I'm going to be a teacher. In a real classroom!"

I was immediately impressed with Jannie. She asked some thoughtful and intelligent questions. And she smiled a lot. In the days that followed, it became increasingly obvious that the children responded to her in a very positive way. I could tell the exact moment when she came into the building. "Miss Jannie's coming," someone would shout, and soon she'd be surrounded by a group of youngsters who wanted to help with her coat, take her books and see that she got to the right room.

I couldn't exactly put my finger on it, but there was something quite special about Jannie. The teachers noted it and commented on how well she was doing. "For a student teacher," they would say, "she seems to have a knack for the job."

Miss Jefferson added, "She could never learn how to relate to the children like she does. No textbook teaches that kind of thing!"

The situation with Thad started, I'm sure, without Jannie's knowledge. Thad was a student in the older class, where they all exhibited only mild mental retardation, but there was a great deal of variation in their abilities and behavior.

Thad was not very articulate, but he was less delayed in other ways. It was my observation that this combination of awareness and inability caused Thad to be frustrated at times and difficult to handle in the classroom. He would retreat for days—not participating, not contributing, not making any effort to be a part of the group.

But soon after Jannie came, Thad began to change. Mrs. Grimes, the regular teacher, was the first to mention it. "Thad Stevens has really been making progress in reading. He's always been reluctant to be a part of the reading groups. But all of a sudden, he's perked up since Jannie has come," she said.

At our next conference, Jannie mentioned Thad with particular pleasure. "I think he's almost ready for a new reader." Then she added with that special Jannie sparkle in her eyes, "I wonder, is there any reason that I couldn't work with him after school a little? He seems so anxious to learn."

"No, Jannie," I told her. "I don't have any objection to individual tutoring if Mrs. Grimes agrees. Maybe Thad finally has found his incentive to learn. Do you suppose you're that incentive?" I asked lightly.

The now serious blue eyes studied me carefully. "I don't know about the incentive, Mrs. McArthur. But I can see that he wants to try. And I don't mind spending the extra time."

Mrs. Grimes agreed and after that, almost daily, Jannie and Thad worked for an hour or so after the regular classes were over. I'd walk by the room and see them—Jannie intent on explaining something, and Thad, more alert and enthusiastic than I'd ever seen him, repeating words and trying to sound out new words he'd never tried before. It was quite beautiful, really.

Some time after that, Gladys Grimes raised the first warning flags. And I was honestly surprised. "He's just crazy about her," she told me, "and I'm concerned because I just don't know what he's going to do when she goes away. He doesn't seem to realize that she won't always be his special teacher. Of course," she said slowly, "he does do well with her. I certainly won't deny that."

"Jannie," I said at our next meeting, "are you aware that Thad is very much attracted to you? He was so different before you came. Now he's reading well and doing other things that he didn't do before. I'm just wondering if you know about Thad's feelings. I'm sure you'd never want to hurt him."

She didn't answer for a moment. She had been looking down and when she raised her eyes, they were puzzled. "Hurt him, Mrs. McArthur? How do you think I could hurt him?"

"By his understanding that you will be going away at the end of the semester and that he probably will never see you again. By the realization that you don't share the kinds of feelings he has for you, my dear."

"But—" she hesitated, "he's been doing so well with the reading. I'm not aware of the kind of feelings I think you mean. It's just—he doesn't have anyone at home to help him," she said. "You probably know that."

I did know, and that made it all the harder. Thad's mother was dead and there were no other children in the family. The father was a seemingly cold, hostile man. We saw very little of him, even at requested conferences or meetings.

"I understand how you feel, Jannie," I said. "I really do. But perhaps you've been giving him too much of your time and attention. If it's something you'd find difficult to handle, maybe you'd like me to talk with him."

"No. No, I don't think so," Jannie said. "But thank you, Mrs. McArthur. I appreciate your concern and I'll let you know if—if I need any help."

My heart went out to Thad when I saw them together. It was obvious that he cared deeply. It was in his eyes as he watched her, in his voice when he spoke to her. I wanted to keep him from being hurt, but I could see it coming. I noticed that the tutoring sessions did taper off a little. But I knew the hurt was inevitable.

The days just before the end of the semester went quickly, and then it was Jannie's final week. There was great excitement about a party for her on the last day. There was singing and a cake, gifts and cards—and some tears, too.

When it was all over and classes had been dismissed, I walked past the classroom. There she was. And Thad was sitting at the back of the room. He had a book in his hand, but it was closed. He was looking at Jannie. I didn't intentionally eavesdrop, but I couldn't help hearing him say, "So you're going away." It was not a question, only a deep, anguished statement of fact.

"Yes," Jannie replied. "And I'm going to miss you all very much."

Thad didn't say anything. He got up from the desk and walked toward her. When he got directly in front of her desk he stood quietly. Jannie raised her eyes and looked back at him for a long moment.

"Miss Jannie . . . Miss Jannie," he began, "I will miss you. You have taught me so much. You have taught me how to read better. And how to be . . . happier . . . here at school. Most of all, Miss Jannie . . ." Only then did his voice begin to quaver. "I have felt how . . . love is." Then he asked politely, "Can I touch your hand . . . to say . . ." He stopped—then, "goodbye?"

Jannie didn't answer. I could see her struggling. The sensitive young chin was trembling and her eyes were blinking very fast. "Of course, Thad," she said. Then she got up, moved around the desk and took both of his hands in hers. "Thank you for telling me. I'm glad you felt that you could. And I'm glad, too, that we have known each other."

Thad didn't answer. As he went out of the room past me he said simply, "She's leaving today."

I nodded. "Yes, I know."

I went into the room then. Jannie was busily cleaning out her desk and arranging things neatly. She didn't look at me right away. And for a long time, there were no words, Finally I said, "He cares a great deal about you."

"And I care about him," she said as the tears spilled over. "I didn't realize how much I cared for all of them—and Thad especially—until it was time to say goodbye. And now—now I wish it didn't hurt so much."

"Perhaps it always hurts at the time, Jannie, if you've left anything of yourself behind—if there were any feelings at all. But the joy of it balances out, I think. Sometimes it takes awhile, though."

She nodded slowly.

"He's never reached out like that before to anyone here," I said. "But you showed him the way. And he'll do it again, Jannie. Because of you."

There have been many student teachers here at Hartwick Center. But the one thing we never can teach them, and the thing they never can learn from a book, is "how love is." Yet it is the single most important part of teaching—of life itself.

And Jannie knew it all the time.

Dorothy Trebilcock

The Eleven O'Clock Appointment

"But Lord," I argued with the small voice within me, "there simply isn't time to drive across town to visit Jake at the hospital and still make my eleven o'clock appointment."

Sheets of rain had translated this spring day into one reminiscent of early fall. Driving in the rain had long been tops on my list of dislikes, and now this heavy city traffic was grating my nerves raw.

The worn–out windshield wipers squeaked with every swipe, providing further aggravation. I've been living outside the city too long, I thought, as a tractor–trailer passed me in a no–passing zone, sending up a wall of water, which momentarily blinded my vision. "Shame on you!" I blurted aloud. "Truck drivers should know better!"

Several unrelated duties had brought me out on this rainy day into the city. As I fiddled with the car radio to get a report of how long this deluge would last, I wished I were back in my small hometown, baking bread in my kitchen or curled up on the couch with a good book.

I remembered a small coffee shop near where I was due to keep my appointment. I recalled its cozy decor and friendly waitresses. I'll buy a magazine at the newsstand and bide my time at the coffee shop until eleven o'clock, I thought, rolling the plan over in my mind. I couldn't wait to get out of this soggy day.

"If you go into town anytime soon," my friend Audrey had said to me on the phone just two days ago, "be sure to stop by the hospital and see Jake and Ella." Her words preyed on my mind as I darted along the busy street toward the coffee shop.

Ella and Audrey are sisters, and Ella's husband, Jake, was now in the final stages of terminal cancer. Audrey and I would often visit Jake and Ella's rural home, where a hospital bed had been set up in their living room. Jake enjoyed listening to us read from the Bible. "Just one more passage," he would say as we attempted to leave.

I shuddered remembering the odor that had developed in Jake's sickly body. Surely, by now it must be worse, and his pallid coloring—well, it was almost more than a person could bear. That, plus all the antiseptic smells of the hospital.

Of course, those reasons weren't keeping me from the hospital, I said to myself as I dashed to the newsstand and chose an appealing magazine. I just don't have time to drive in this horrid rain clear across town and get back for my eleven o'clock appointment.

The coffee shop was as friendly as I had remembered it. I found a corner booth far from the rain–streaked windows so I could forget the downpour. "I have never liked driving in the rain," I muttered to the waitress as I ordered hot coffee and a roll. She agreed heartily that rainy streets were very dangerous, and the best thing to do is get in somewhere and wait it out.

"See there, Lord?" I said to the small voice inside. "Besides, it's twenty minutes 'til ten, and I couldn't possibly make it over there and back in time—or could I?"

I was now thoroughly exasperated with myself. I seemed to have a full–blown case of the fidgets. There was a compulsion within me that was too strong to be ignored, no matter how legitimate my excuses.

So I worked it out in my head: Let's see, thirty minutes to drive to the hospital, twenty minutes to visit, and thirty to get back. If I leave right this minute, I just might make it.

I couldn't believe I was leaving the warmth of the cozy coffee shop to go back into the chilly dampness. As I hastily paid the bill and left, I caught a glimpse of the waitress staring at my half–eaten roll and the unread magazine lying on the table.

Jake's room was lit only by the filtered light pressing in through the window from the gray day. Ella was seated by the window, her fingers busily crocheting a rainbow afghan in the muted light. I watched her shrouded in that warm glow. Neatly dressed, with every hair in place, her face reflected peace. But as she looked up and noticed me at the door, there were tears glistening in her eyes. She rose to greet me and invited me to come in and sit down. Jake was sleeping fitfully.

Ella shared bits of news from the latest reports. Then she said, "The Lord is so faithful to send someone to me when I think I cannot go on another moment. Thank you for coming." I had no words.

The rain continued to play its patter on the tall window, sending droplets streaking down the pane. "The sound of the rain is God's beautiful melody, isn't it?" she said softly.

"Yes, I know," I said, but I didn't really know. I had been irritated by the simple sound of squeaking windshield wipers.

At what point had I strayed from the path of a quiet and settled spirit where Ella now walked?

Ella needed to talk, and I listened. She spoke of future plans that must be made. She faced them squarely.

I looked at my watch. Half past ten. "I'd better go," I whispered, rising from my chair. But Jake stirred and saw me.

"Hey there," he said weakly, but with obvious joy. "You come all the way up here just to read me the Bible?"

I started to say I didn't have a Bible, but Ella pressed a small New Testament into my hand.

I began to read. It was now a quarter 'til eleven, but time had ceased to matter.

"Just one more passage?" Jake said sweetly, "You may think I'm asleep," he smiled with eyes closed, "but I'm hearing every word."

Now Ella stood on the opposite side of the bed holding Jake's thin, vein–swollen hand.

"Streets of gold," Jake whispered, referring to the passage in Revelations. "Crystal sea . . ." There was a slight gasp in his voice.

I rang for the nurse, who busied over Jake for a moment. Then she shook her head soberly and drew up the sheet. Ella's tear–filled eyes met mine, and she smiled.

I glanced at my watch—it was eleven o'clock! I had not missed my appointment.

Norma Jean Lutz

The Pelican Easter

She woke to the barest hint of light behind the curtains. On the beach beyond, a pelican sat, still as the morning, among graceful gulls and terns. The night had been warm, yet a slight shiver crept down from her head and lodged somewhere in her chest.

Todd sighed as she eased away. "Vi?" he mouthed with closed eyes, then rolled over, asleep again.

Vi dressed, smiled at Todd's strong body curled as vulnerably as a child's, and slipped out the door of the beachfront cottage.

They had chosen this strip of beach on Tampa Bay for its beauty and seclusion. Sea oats, still silvery from the embrace of moonlight, waved in the pre–dawn mist, and white sand stretched in a grand sweep to the shore.

It was her name that had fascinated Todd in the beginning, but he had agreed to call her Vi, rather than Venus, as she had been officially named. Hardly a goddess of love, Vi had wandered into more than one disappointing relationship, then married Will. She had hoped then that the hollow irony of her birthright was ended, but it was her marriage that later ended, instead.

Now two years after her divorce, and in the midst of a busy professional career, Vi was taking a spring vacation with Todd Bayley. They had been dating sporadically, then when cold January swept into frigid February, something had sparked their easy friendship. She now loved him fiercely and, without hesitation, had said yes to this week.

"I know it's the twenty–first century, Vi, but this isn't like you." Her friend Corrine's voice echoed now in her ears.

No, it wasn't like her. But nothing was anymore, not since losing Will. They had thought their strong church roots and commitment to family values would keep them together. But one April day two years past he had quietly informed her it was over.

"I'm sorry, I just can't do this anymore." Will's husky pronouncement had finished the downward spiral of their five–year marriage. That there had been no children was now blessing rather than bane.

When she had finished her petulant protest to God, she had picked up the pieces and gone on—even remaining active in her Bible study group. But she avoided this One who once had been the center of her faith. It had to be His fault that inside she felt as cold as a tombstone. Until Todd. She loved him for making her feel wanted, needed. He had been patient, and she had finally said yes.

Now it was more than guilt that drove her onto the beach on Easter morning. It was the overwhelming sense that, in spite of Todd's love, she was not yet alive.

"I'll make you happy, Vi. I swear I will." Todd had meant it. It was wrong of her to make him think he could.

Pink ribbons of sunlight were spreading rapidly along the horizon, and Vi realized she was near the marshy area where she had worked as a college student with a local environmental group to save certain endangered birds from industrial pollutants.

The beach was deserted. Vi recalled as a half–remembered dream other Easter mornings, other sunrise services. She had looked for Him in the quiet prayers, the drama and the music. But this year was different, of course. Todd was waiting for her; they would have breakfast at the Island Inn and spend the day on the beach. She wasn't looking for anything else. She watched the water stop just short of her sandalled feet. A sudden, sad epiphany signaled her utter detachment.

Then Vi heard a rustling in the reeds before she saw the gray–white pelican with one wing awkwardly thrashing in the thicket, its long bill pecking at a tangle of weeds and feathers. Vi dropped to the ground. Shivering in her shorts and beach jacket, she peered through the tall weeds.

The pelican hobbled weakly, shuffling its ungainly body. A wing was clotted with a dark, sticky substance, and one foot was virtually glued to its left–wing feathers. It pecked the sticky mass, eyes glossy with fright or exhaustion.

Vi had seen this before. The pelican would die without help. With sudden inspiration, she raced back to the cottage and rifled through her suitcase for the rubbing alcohol. It was a poor substitute, but its chemical properties in diluted form were similar to the compound she had used in college.

Todd raised himself on one elbow, sleep and puzzlement marking his handsome features.

"Go back to sleep." She gave him a fond smile and on impulse reached for her bottle of oily nail polish remover. "I'm going for a run before breakfast, okay?"

As the skies spilled their gold and crimson wine, she hurried back to the marsh. The bay was blue–green and bilious with sky, and she felt sudden intoxication. "I'm coming," she whispered as she sped to the spot.

The pelican was quieter now, but as she approached, it began to thrash about once more. Then it stopped suddenly and looking straight ahead regarded her with one glazed eye.

She grabbed its bill firmly and quickly tied the cord of her beach jacket around the hard bony beak. Then pinning the bird between her knees and cajoling softly she went to work. She felt the bird's quick, wild pulse against her thigh.

"Dear God," she whispered, then laughed in soft irony. She couldn't act on faith to get her own life together, and here she was praying over a dumb bird! *Could it be true that He really cared about both of them?*

As she worked, the bird gradually grew quieter. Had the process been too much? Had she killed the pelican? Panic and pain engulfed her in simultaneous waves. *It must live. Please God.* She waited, then relaxed her hold on all but the dangerous beak.

Suddenly the pelican fanned out its full wing feathers and began a wild fluttering dance. When its energy was spent, she released the cord from the bird's beak and ran. Several yards away, from the safety of a stand of reeds and brush, she watched the pelican take several stumbling steps. Then with a mighty sweep of wing it soared out across the water.

Sunlight touched its wings, transforming them into an exquisite white cross rising into the clouds. Deeper and deeper into the golden horizon it soared until it became one with the heavens and with every suffering soul who sought release.

The sun permeated Vi's face and body. She lay flat in the warm sand and stretched her arms out as though to embrace the love that had nailed the Lord of heaven to a cross. Love that she had alternately craved and denied. How could she explain it—the sense that God had somehow come to her? That she, too, could be alive and free?

She felt the tears spill over onto the sand, as in an inaudible rush she poured out her long, sullen silence before the God of the Easter sunrise.

Lt. Colonel Marlene Chase

Rebirth

On the week before Easter, Mrs. Johnson said to her Sunday school class, "Today is Palm Sunday, and next Sunday is Easter. Jesus rose from the dead on Easter. As we think of Jesus rising from the dead, we think of rebirth, of dead things coming to life again. Like the grass that withers and dies in the fall but in the springtime is reborn. Next week on Easter Sunday, I would like you to bring something to class that symbolizes rebirth."

Hers was a small class of five students. One of them, Josh, had mild mental retardation, and the teacher was not always sure how much of the lesson he understood. Sometimes, outside of the Sunday School class, other children would make fun of him.

So, to be sure that Josh would not be embarrassed if he did not bring the right thing, she asked each child to bring his or her item in an unmarked box, put them on her desk, and she would open them herself and show them to the class.

Easter Sunday came and there were five boxes on the teacher's desk. She began to open them. Inside the first box was an egg.

Mary raised her hand to identify her box. "When I think of eggs hatching and becoming little chickens, I think that is rebirth."

"Thank you, Mary, the egg is a very good symbol of birth and new life," complimented the teacher. Then she opened the second box, and inside was a flower.

Susie, bursting with pride, said, "Mrs. Johnson, that's my flower. Mommy grows beautiful flowers in our yard. She puts seeds and old bulbs in the ground and they grow into beautiful flowers. That reminds me of rebirth."

"Thank you, Susie. Flowers are beautiful signs of rebirth," said Mrs. Johnson. The teacher opened the third box and inside was a rock. "Jimmy, did you bring this rock?"

"Yes, Mrs. Johnson," he replied.

"Well how does this rock symbolize rebirth?" asked his teacher.

"Because moss is growing on the rock, and there is life growing on what's dead," he replied.

"Thank you Jimmy. That's a very thoughtful example," said his teacher in praise of his good idea.

Inside the fourth box was a beautiful butterfly. The teacher knew this must have come from Bill's butterfly collection.

Bill said, "When I look at a butterfly, I think of a caterpillar; and when he makes his cocoon, and then his shell dies, he comes out as a butterfly in the spring. That reminds me of rebirth."

"That's very good, Bill." said Mrs. Johnson. "The butterfly is one of the most lovely examples of rebirth. Some people use the butterfly as a symbol of the resurrection."

The teacher hesitated as she opened the fifth box, knowing it would have come from Josh. She peeked inside and then quickly closed it and started to set it down. But she heard Josh's voice saying, "Mrs. Johnson, please open my box. Don't leave it out."

Mrs. Johnson answered, "But Josh, your box is empty."

"That's right, Mrs. Johnson," said Josh. "That's because the tomb of Jesus was empty on Easter Sunday when He rose from the dead. And the empty tomb tells us Jesus brought life out of death."

Mrs. Johnson paused in silence for what seemed like long moments. Her students noticed her eyes were wet with tears. She knew her student Josh had understood the beautiful meaning of Easter.

When she was finally able to speak, Mrs. Johnson said, "Thank you Josh. You have really caught the meaning of Easter. Your empty box is a beautiful lesson and reminder to all of us that the real meaning of Easter is that Jesus rose from the dead. Out of His death came life, not only for Himself but for all of us. Because of His resurrection on Easter Sunday, we may all have new and beautiful life—not only here in this world, but forever with Him in Heaven. Thank you Josh for helping us understand the true meaning of Easter."

The other four members of Mrs. Johnson's class congratulated Josh on his excellent idea.

Jimmy said, "Your empty box was the greatest idea of all. I wish I had thought of that!"

Major Helen Johnson

Life Time

Protests patterned themselves upon his mind, but each new thought replaced its predecessor as relentlessly as the rain reappeared in front of his eyes against the rhythmic objections of the windshield wipers.

A man of sixty–eight had time left, he tried to convince himself, even though a fifty–two–year stint with a single company would end on Friday. "Time is money," he had always heard it said, but a man alone had little use for such riches. And no other corporation courted his personal investment.

The rain–slicked road demanded his attention now. Frowning, he slowed to negotiate a series of snake turns above the river. The first time he had encountered these curves he'd pedaled his bicycle along the upgrade. Sixteen and strong, eager to do a man's work, he'd arrived at the mill so breathless that he had barely managed to choke out his name. The timekeeper, signing on employees for the new industry, hadn't understood. Finally, he had spelled it out: B–E–N–H–A–M, John. That half century seemed only a moment.

Then his throat tightened as he saw a tiny foreign car skid around the curve ahead and come bearing down on his truck. His fingers tightened around the steering wheel.

John searched for an escape path, already aware that none existed. To the left, a bluff rose sharply from a narrow shoulder. Opposite, the drop to the river. This was a steer–and–pray situation. He'd had some experience in both, but more in the former.

And then, when neither action seemed effective, the aggressor veered sharply. From the corner of his eye and then the side mirror, John watched the car's descent and the spray of displaced water.

John's foot pumped the brake petal—gently, repeatedly—until the truck eased itself to the meager gravel strip and idled, awaiting his next impulse. He began by wishing that another car would come this way. Then he shut off the engine and jammed a rain hat down on his balding head.

Years ago one could hope for traffic and get it, but that was when the mill centered the thriving community of Sawyer. Now the maintained road ended just beyond the mill, which had been scheduled for obsolescence. It was no longer necessary to go upriver from Titusville unless one happened to be John Benham, assigned the final tasks of boarding up the windows and doors and hauling away the trash.

Rain drummed on his oilskins as he slid down the slope through the grass and low bushes. The rocks at the river's edge, underwater now during spring's engorgement, wore a greenish, slimy substance.

The car had flipped to its side, driver's–door–up, so that its roof pressed against a downstream deadfall. Next to the underframing, the river beat itself into waves.

"Hello there!"

Only pounding water answered. Perhaps the occupants could not detect his voice. A pool of quiet water lay between John and the vehicle. He approached it with distrust.

In years past he'd fought the Titus River for its treasure of trout. Martha had a special way of frying fish, he remembered. But, as often as not, lured into a hidden hole or off a precarious ledge, he'd caught cold as well as his limit of trout.

Reluctantly John shrugged off his slicker and folded it, keeping the dry inner surfaces together. If necessary, he'd fight off his boots later. After three steps forward he paused to accustom his toes to the chill sponging in through thick woolen socks. Like an otter seeking its rock, John slithered onto the rear of the car.

Breaking water slapped his face. Perhaps, as they did with men, the years were also turning the Titus colder. He shook his head impatiently to clear his eyes. He could not spare a hand for wiping.

Frustration jabbed at him as his fingers, stiff and unwilling, fumbled with the latch. "Don't hang up, you fool door! Not now! "

A combination of pushing and lifting freed it. He threw the panel away from him, so far that the door stood erect on its pins.

And there she was—suspended in the upper portion of the compartment by her seatbelt, hands clenched on the wheel. Water appeared to be her only companion. Slowly her face turned toward his. Thin, pale lips spread to speak.

"Someone came," a small voice marveled. "You came."

He reached to free her buckle and found it overlaid with layers of sodden wool. Considering the tiny head, the woman was surprisingly large. "Chubby" was the word Martha had always favored.

His strength and control surprised even John. With the movements of a younger, surer man, he pulled the girl up and guided her to the back of the car.

"Were any children with you?" He thrust his mouth close to her ear so she would hear.

Her head swayed. One hand pressed against her middle.

"My child is here. I must get to the hospital."

The desperation in her voice sent John vaulting into the knee–deep pool. He reached back and swept the girl to the bank where he shrouded her in the waiting oilskin. As an afterthought, he clawed the hat from his head to set it atop the straggling black hair.

Some heat still remained in the cab when he boosted her inside and tucked the trailing layers of coats around her thin, shaking legs. Before pulling out onto the road, he cranked open the heater vents.

"Is . . . are you . . . is it your time?" Funny how far back in memory that phrase was tucked, last used forty years ago.

"I don't know." Her voice wavered. "There wasn't anyone to ask, and the phone wouldn't work. The rain, I guess."

"You're from around here? How come you turned toward Sawyer?"

The way he'd always handled Martha's labor was to ask questions during the entire trip.

She responded by asking, "Isn't that where the hospital is? I mean, this is Sawyer County." She watched him shake his head. "I've only been here three weeks. I live with the Ortegas."

"Know of them," he offered. So did most of the old timers, he supposed. Joe Ortega Sr., a migrant farm laborer, had arrived one summer to work the valley's fruit crop. But he was a shrewd man who saved well. When the other migrant workers climbed aboard their rusted–out buses heading toward the next harvest, Joe stayed to raise grapes and children. "Young Joe made basketball All–State a couple of years ago. My boy did, too, back in forty–one."

"Jose's in Vietnam," she whispered. "I was staying with my sister in Los Angeles before, but things didn't work out. So Mama and Papa Ortega asked me to come here."

"And they left you alone?"

"I told them it was all right. Papa's brother died and they had to go to the funeral, you know. They'll be back day after tomorrow." She curled forward, grasping the dashboard.

"The hospital at Titusville is real fine," he told her. "Both my kids were born there."

"I might be wrong about the baby." Doubt clouded her speech. "But it was so awful being alone. My name is Anita."

"I am John Benham. And that's the hospital down below."

Titusville General was where he'd first learned about being alone. Five years ago all his plans for retirement had ended—because every project, all the trips, had included Martha.

"Can you hurry, please?" The girl's shrill cry reverberated within the compartment.

"Not on these roads. But I know some shortcuts," John said.

In her quest to find a hospital, Anita Ortega had put herself in the hands of an expert. During the two months of driving to see Martha twice each day, John had sought alternate routes in a frantic attempt to change the routine and its inevitable end. But he would not tell Anita of this. Death was not an apt subject in the presence of new life. He stopped the truck in front of the emergency entrance.

"We're here, Anita."

"You'll stay with me, please? I couldn't bear to be alone again." She scrambled clumsily from the cab and clung to him.

Just inside the door, attendants gently untangled her fingers from his windbreaker, then he watched her disappear down the hall. Anita would never know if he didn't remain at the hospital, he thought. And she certainly would not be left alone now in her condition.

Still, the staff should be told about the accident. It might make a difference in how they handled things. Besides, he knew a place in the lobby where the heating system blew directly on a person, and the basement cafeteria served a decent meal.

So he talked to Mrs. Moore in the admissions office. She remembered him from before. After phoning her information to Maternity, she located a pair of slippers. His boots and socks were set to steam on the register behind her desk.

The food tasted better than he had remembered, and the lobby blower still held true aim. In due time he dozed.

"Mr. Benham! John Benham!"

He awoke with a start.

Mrs. Moore stood in front of him. "Mother and son are doing fine. Mrs. Ortega would like to see you."

He pushed himself up from his chair and moved quickly down the newly polished corridor. The announcement of a new life pleased him. But more than that—a deep feeling of personal renewal filled his heart. Suddenly he was positive that his retirement years could have worth and meaning. For there would be others, like Anita, who were driven by the fears which loneliness brought.

John Benham bent down beside the bed so that he might hear more clearly those words of wonder and gratitude that Anita's smiling lips now formed.

"You came! I'm so glad."

Marilyn Jakes Church

Resurrection Morning

"Tell it again, you say? Tell it again? I've told you all I know. I've even told you what I don't know."

"But some are just arriving. They haven't heard what you saw. Tell us again."

The heavy door opened and shut quickly as two more men entered the small room. Claudius supposed this was a storage room, but he wasn't sure. It was too dark. The only light was a slit of afternoon sunshine creeping through an opening in the wooden shutters and streaking across the faces of the listeners.

The group numbered fifteen, maybe twenty—about as many men as women. A few men were shaven, most bearded. A few asked questions. A few shook their heads. All sat with eyes fixed on the young soldier whose story they longed to hear but didn't know whether to believe.

Claudius took a breath and began his story again. "I wasn't supposed to work that night. I'd worked over the Sabbath and was tired. In fact, I bad been on duty since Friday morning."

"I remember your face." The voice belonged to a woman sitting on the floor. "You were on the hill."

"I was assigned the Golgotha detail a month ago." A grumble went up from the group. Claudius defended himself, "I didn't ask for it—I was given it." Emotion was thick in the room, but then someone was urging, "Go on, finish the story!"

Claudius again shifted his weight. He would never have imagined himself in a room full of Jews. The contrast between his trimmed hair and short uniform and their beards and robes only added to his discomfort. He eyed his spear on the floor at his feet. His Roman shield leaned against the adobe wall. Coming here was a dangerous move.

He had been uneasy ever since he had arrived in Jerusalem a few months back. It certainly wasn't his choice of a place to serve, but when Rome sends, a soldier obeys. Besides, he told himself, a year in a peaceful outpost couldn't be too bad.

Wrong. Jerusalem was far from peaceful. The Jews hated the soldiers. The soldiers distrusted the Jews. If it wasn't the priest's complaints, it was the zealots' riots. Jerusalem was a hotbed of anger. Anger at Rome. Anger at the world.

They called themselves the people of God. Some nation of God! No navy. Puny army. No emperor. Just a Temple, a Torah and some strange rules about the Sabbath. Claudius had been trained to respect strength and size—neither of which he found here.

Until last night. What he saw last night he'd never seen in Rome or anywhere else. When he told his officers about it, they told him to keep quiet. He couldn't. He had to have some answers. So he came here.

These people wanted answers, too. So they let him in. They were easy to find. Every soldier in the city knew where they were hiding—the upper room of the large white corner house. It was the same place they had met last week when He was still there.

When Claudius learned how they had run away and left Him alone, he was amazed that they had returned. "Why are you still here then?" he had asked. "Why don't you go home?"

"If you'd seen Him do what we've seen Him do, you would stay, too," a disciple explained.

"Sounds like he has," said another.

"When I first saw Him being led up the hill, I noticed that He was different. He didn't demand that we let Him go. He didn't shout or resist. And when we hammered the spike into His hand," Claudius paused, wondering if he should have mentioned this. An encouraging nod from one of the women told him to continue. "When we placed the spike into His hand, He held His hand still. He didn't fight."

He continued. "'Forgive them,' I heard Him say. And when He spoke, I looked up. He was looking at me. His face was a mask of blood and spit. But He was praying for me." The only movement in the room was nodding heads.

"After the crucifixion, I helped lower the body onto the ground. I waited as these women—" he motioned to several women near the front. "I waited as they prepared the body, and then I saw that it was placed in the tomb.

"I thought my day was over. It took four men to close the grave's opening with a huge stone. When we turned to leave, word came that Pilate and the Temple leaders were nervous that someone would steal the body. We were told to seal the tomb and stand guard all night.

"There were several of us, so we built a fire and took turns. I was the first to sleep. When they woke me for my turn, it was an hour before dawn. The night was black—as black as any night I can remember.

"I stood on one side. Another soldier stood on the other. He laughed about how easy it was to guard a tomb. Not often does a soldier get guard duty in a cemetery. Maybe we dozed off because at first I thought I was dreaming. The ground began to shake—violently. It shook so hard I fell to the ground. The soldiers asleep on the ground jumped up. I know they were standing because when the light hit them, I could see their faces like it was broad daylight.

"What light?" someone asked. "You tell me!" Claudius demanded. "Where did that light come from? The rock rolled back and the light roared out. A burst of fire with no heat. A gust of wind blew from the tomb, put out the fire, knocked us back, and the next thing I knew, the tomb was empty. I looked at the soldiers. They were stunned. About that time these two women appeared."

"That's when we saw the angel!" Mary blurted. "He was sitting on the rock! He told us Jesus was not here. He told us that . . ."

She hesitated, knowing her words would be hard to believe.

"He told us Jesus is no longer dead!" Her words rang like the peal of a bell. No one dared speak. Finally one did. A clean–shaven younger man said softly, "Just like He said He would."

"You mean, He said He would do this?" Claudius asked.

"More than once. But we didn't understand. Until today."

Once again the room was quiet. Then Claudius broke the silence.

"I have a question. I've told you what you wanted to know. Now you tell me what I want to know. This has been on my mind all weekend. It's been on my heart ever since I struck the nail into Jesus' hand. Who is this man? Who is this Jesus?"

"Is there any doubt?" Mary said. Her eyes were bright. She jumped to her feet as she spoke. "I saw Him! I saw Him risen from the dead! He is who He said He was. He is the Son of God!"

With that statement the room broke into chaos.

"Impossible."

"No, she is right. Let her speak!"

"Why did He let them kill Him. If He is the Son of God?"

"It doesn't make sense."

"What doesn't make sense is why you can't believe!"

Claudius was silent. What he was hearing, he could not handle. But what he had seen at the grave, he could not deny. He leaned over and put his elbows on his knees and buried his face in his hands. Thoughts rumbled in his head. He was so intent on his thoughts that he didn't notice the sudden stillness. When he raised his head, he noticed light filling the room.

Faces that had been cast in shadows now beamed. All eyes stared in his direction—not at him, but behind him. Before he could turn to see what they were seeing, a hand was on his shoulder. When Claudius turned to look at the hand, he found the answer for his heart.

The hand was pierced.

Max Lucado

From *Tell Me the Story* by Max Lucado, ©1991, pgs. 18–23. Used by permission of Good News Publishers/Crossway Books, Wheaton, Illinois 60187.

CREST BOOKS

Salvation Army National Publications

Crest Books, a division of The Salvation Army's National Publications department, was established in 1997 so contemporary Salvationist voices could be captured and bound in enduring form for future generations, to serve as witnesses to the continuing force and mission of the Army.

Never the Same Again
by Shaw Clifton

Clifton encourages new believers' enthusiasm for Christ and guides them through road-blocks that stunt spiritual growth. An ideal resource for new converts, seekers looking to know more about the Christian faith, as well as leaders of discipling groups.

Christmas Through the Years:
A War Cry Treasury

Contains the articles, stories, poems, and art that have inspired our readers for over half a century. This treasury highlights Salvationists of wide appeal and features contributors such as Billy Graham and Joni Eareckson Tada.

Celebrate the Feasts of the Lord
by William W. Francis

A historical examination of the feasts and fasts established by God in Leviticus 23. This book meets a critical need by revealing how Jesus participated in the feasts and how, in Himself, their meaning was fulfilled. Study guides follow each chapter.

Easter Through the Years:
A War Cry Treasury

Recounts the passion of Christ and the events surrounding the cross, reminding us of the numerous ways Easter intersects with our lives and faith today. Spend some time with contributors such as Max Lucado and General William Booth.

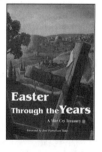

Slightly Off Center!
by Terry Camsey

An expert in the field of church health, Camsey urges us to welcome the new generation of Salvationists. The methods may be different, but their hearts are wholly God's and their mission remains consistent with the fundamental principles William Booth established.

A Little Greatness
by Joe Noland

Readers explore the book of Acts, revealing the paradoxes of the life of a believer. Noland examines the story of the early Church and reveals its relevance today. A Bible study and discussion guide for each chapter makes this an ideal group study resource.

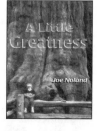

Romance & Dynamite:
Essays on Science and the Nature of Faith
by Lyell M. Rader

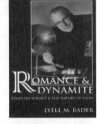

Anecdotes and insights on the interplay of science and faith by one of the Army's most indefatigable evangelists. The author uses his training as a chemist to prove the trustworthiness of the Bible and demonstrate why the saving knowledge of God is crucial to understanding life's value and purpose.

He Who Laughed First:
Delighting in a Holy God
by Phil Needham

The author questions why so many sour-faced saints exist when Christian life is meant to be joyful. He explores the secret to enduring joy, a joy that is found by letting God make us holy, by letting Him free us to become who we are in Christ—saints. Discover the why and how of becoming a joyful, hilarious saint.

Pictures from the Word
by Marlene Chase

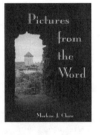

"The Bible is full of beautiful word pictures, concrete images that bring to life spiritual ideas," writes Chase. The author brings to life the vivid metaphors of Scripture, while illuminating familiar passages and addressing frequent references to the vulnerability of man met by God's limitless and gracious provision.

If Two Shall Agree
by Carroll Ferguson Hunt

The fascinating story of how God brought Paul and Kay Rader together and melded them into a team that served in The Salvation Army for over thirty-five years. Follow their journey and their vision. See the power and far-reaching influence of a couple who serve together as one in the name of Christ.

Who Are These Salvationists?
by Shaw Clifton

This study explores the Army's roots, theology and position in the body of believers, offering a definitive profile of what is salvationism. Salvationists are aided in their understanding of the Army's mission in the twenty-first century and non-Salvationists are introduced to the theology that drives its social action. The most comprehensive portrait of the Army to date.

Our God Comes:
And Will Not Be Silent
by Marlene Chase

This book of poetry rests on the premise that, like the unstoppable ocean tide, God comes to us in a variety of ways, and His voice is never silenced as He is heard throughout all Creation. Ideal for small group discussion and devotional meditation, as well as literary enjoyment of carefully crafted poetry.

A Salvationist Treasury
edited by Henry Gariepy

Colonel Henry Gariepy brings together the devotional writings by Salvationist authors spanning a hundred years. These inspirational readings will enrich your spiritual life, deepen your biblical study, and enhance 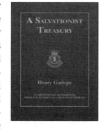 your grasp of the Army's principles and mission. A milestone compilation of Army literature.

Pen of Flame: The Life and Poetry of Catherine Baird
by John C. Izzard with Henry Gariepy

As a poet, hymn writer, and editor, Catherine Baird changed the way The Salvation Army viewed the importance of the written word. From a decade of research and devotion, Izzard has painted a compelling picture of one  of the Army's strongest yet most delicate authors.

Fractured Parables
by A. Kenneth Wilson

The people of the Bible are as real as we are today. Major Wilson demonstrates this by holding beloved biblical accounts up to the light of modernity. By recasting Jesus' parables in contemporary circumstances and language, 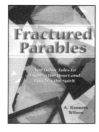 the author reveals gems of truth in earthly guise. His knack for finding humor in the mundane will also lighten your heart.

Andy Miller: A Legend and a Legacy
by Henry Gariepy

This biography by Colonel Gariepy seeks, through anecdotes, to convey the story of one of the most colorful and remarkable leaders in the history of the Army. As an American Salvationist, Andy Miller has had a powerful 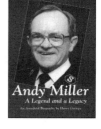 spiritual impact on innumerable lives, both within and outside the ranks.
